I AM HOLDING YOUR HAND

STORIES

MYFANWY COLLINS

PANK
BOOKS

PUBLISHED BY [PANK]
Houghton, MI
http://www.pankmagazine.com

Copyright © 2012 Myfanwy Collins

Cover and Book Design by Alban Fischer

ISBN: 978-0-9824697-9-8
First Edition

CONTENTS

I
AM
HOLDING
YOUR
HAND

I
AM
HOLDING
YOUR
HAND

It was Christmas Eve and Jessie was hallucinating. She was ten and her tonsils were infected, but she would not be one of the lucky ones who had the operation to remove the dangling bits. She would not be one of the lucky ones who got live on post-op ice cream. No, she would suffer through with the help of antibiotics. Her tonsils would not have a chance to grow back.

Jessie's mother had her tonsils removed as a girl, but they grew back, a fact Jessie found both disturbing and titillating. That humans might have body parts which grew back. Could this mean there was a cure for death?

When she was much older Jessie would be on a subway with a fellow from Germany. He would tell her how his body had become covered in lumps when he was nineteen. Upon investigation the doctors found that the lumps contained hair and bone and teeth. He had absorbed his own twin while he was in the womb.

But Jessie had no twin, absorbed or otherwise.

Her throat ached, her fever spiked. It was the first year her father was not there on Christmas Eve channeling Louis Armstrong on their way back from Midnight Mass. Instead, he was in his apartment across town. Earlier in the day he'd had the girls over and brought them one after the other into the bathroom and showed them the presents he had gotten for each. Jessie's big sister would receive a stuffed kangaroo, which Jessie coveted. It was small, its fur velveteen. She thought it would work nicely with her Barbies. They might travel to Australia. Skipper might meet a priest in the Outback. Fall in love.

Jessie would spend Christmas day on the couch, sweating, seeing things that were not there, listening to her mother play the new Neil Diamond record over and over until it seemed Neil Diamond had been absorbed into their living room and family.

When her father came, he would bring her a present. A Bert, but no Ernie. Bert was not too much smaller than she was, his head pointy, his clothes removable, but best not removed as underneath he was featureless—a stuffed pillow.

Bert was old. A grown man. What an odd choice. His expression was curmudgeonly, unlovable. She feigned appreciation, though her only feeling toward Bert was pity. He was like her father now, living a life without the company of women.

Her father would die in May, in the night and alone, with not even Ernie by his side to hold his hand, to tell him to hold on. No Ernie to remind him of those times when he was loved.

Remember when you were a boy? You had a white pony and a wide-brimmed hat. Think about that pony, that hat. Focus. I am holding your hand.

THE NEST

The child sleeps in a cluster of blankets they call the nest. Simply, he falls asleep when he falls asleep. They eat dinner when they are hungry. Same for breakfast. Same for lunch.

The nest smells of curdled milk and crusty ears. It smells of piney breath and blackened toes. The child sucks on the frayed satin-edge of a wool blanket. The blanket belonged, long ago, to his grandmother. Then to his mother. Now to him.

The child chews his nails. His scalp is often itchy. He feels compelled to move, always to move. In sleep, his eyes twitch, hands shake, legs shudder. He dreams of polar bears swimming, endlessly swimming, looking for ice or land. The seals are too fast to catch in the water. The polar bears move inward.

The polar bears search the garbage heap for sustenance and find nothing but a small boy asleep in his nest. The boy does not scream when they nose his damp skin. One of them licks his cheek. Another bites off a piece of his foot. He does not scream because he would like to die this way.

Above, stars stab through the black sky, forming the shape of nest and boy.

THE DAUGHTERS

Their mother never teaches them to wipe front to back or to brush their teeth before bed. One of the daughters goes for weeks without washing her hair until the teacher complains that she smells of their father's cigarette smoke.

Their mother does teach them that if they wear their underpants two days in a row they will get sick.

*

The daughters take baths together and wash each other's backs. One, one, one in a line and then turn when each back is done. Turn and turn until their backs are rubbed raw.

*

The daughters learn to clean the dishes with a dishrag, not a sponge. They learn that it is okay to keep butter out so that their toast tastes rancid, even when they cover it in cinnamon.

And they learn that it is fine to have multiple bottles of condiments open in the fridge. Once they count four bottles of ketchup in different stages of use with a skin of red oozing beneath each cap. There is always a scab on top of the plastic mustard container.

*

Their father cleans their ears with an unraveled paper clip. If one is not handy, then he uses the cap of a Bic pen. He squishes one of the daughters next to him on the couch, folds her head down over his lap. He digs at her earwax while he watches the hockey game.

The daughters are not fond of this practice but do not complain. They lie across their father's lap and listen to the aching scratchiness of metal against cartilage. Every so often their father forgets what he's doing and digs too deeply and the daughters flinch.

Stay still, he warns. I could slip and hurt you.

When he is done and the daughters are free to go the inside of their ears tingle red. The sounds of the world seem muted to them, seem dense.

WHAT
HE
TOLD
ME

1

When I was a little kid, Poppy and I hiked up the mountain every spring, before the black flies came out and after the snow melted and ran down to feed the hungry lake. At the top, we rested, ate peanut butter sandwiches with the crust cut off, and drank cold water from a thermos as we sat under the rusting fire tower and scanned the gray-skinned trees not yet filled out by leaves.

Once, on our way back down, we saw a big black dog standing in the middle of the trail below us. I wanted to run ahead and touch it, but Poppy stopped me. "That's a bear, Paula." Poppy took my hand in his and bent down next to me, leaned in close, and whispered as we watched the bear snuffing at the ground. I tilted my head up to Poppy's face—the skin of his cheek next to my nose smelled like the roadside on a hot August day when the rain starts—tender wild roses and dusty leaves, hot tar and sweet clover. What he told me was about bears. Not the little kid stories I knew about honey pots and beds being too hard or too soft. What he told me was the truth.

"You hold onto this, Kid," Poppy said. "You never know when you might need it." The bear went back through the woods without even noticing that we watched him, but I never forgot what Poppy told me: Take your time. Observe. Once you've figured out what you're dealing with, you're safe to move on down the path.

2

Usually Jeannie was allowed to take the boat out by herself but when she brought me into her kitchen, both of us in bikinis and cut-offs and said to her dad, "I'm teaching Paula to ski," he turned from where he was leaning against the counter eating a grilled cheese and looked at us and shook his head. He looked at me. It was quick, the way he looked, but I felt it. I was in a new suit—silver and shiny—that I had bought with the money Aunt May had given me for my fifteenth birthday.

"No, you ain't," he said and popped the crust of his sandwich in his mouth, wiped his hands on his barn jeans. "I'll teach her."

I had a hard time getting up on those skis. Fell over without even getting out of the water and one time forgot to let go of the rope and got dragged on my belly, mouth open like a dumb fish taking in water.

"We'll try one more time," he said, as I bobbed in the cool lake. "Use your upper arms." He pulled his arms up to his chest, slowly as though lifting a dumbbell. "Got it?" he asked. I nodded and tucked my chin under the water and blew bubbles to cover my smile.

Jeannie sat in the front of the boat, wrapped in a towel, pouting. She wanted to be the one giving me instructions. That's the way it was between the two of us, her teaching and me learning. Like how to French kiss. She had pushed my lips open with her small tongue and let it tickle all of my teeth.

I thought about kissing her dad as he leaned over the back of the boat. What it would be like. His moustache. His strong arms around me. I wanted to get up on those skis. For him.

I situated the rope between the skis, the bar tight in my hands and yelled out, "Hit it." As the boat plunged forward, I thought of his arms lifting me out of the water, pulling me up like God pulling Jesus into heaven. And it worked. I was standing but my sodden bottoms were saggy in the crotch and slid down my thin hips. I clamped my thighs together to stop them, but, as I did, my legs wobbled and my calf tightened into a knot of pain.

I felt that I windmilled halfway across the lake and by the time they spun around to get me, Jeannie was laughing so hard that her face was red and puckered. Her dad frowned in concern. "You all right, girl?" he asked.

I nodded and held up a shaking hand, holding my bottoms up with the other. He took my hand and pulled me out of the water into the boat, like I was nothing, like I was Jesus. I sat dripping on the floor and held out my cramped leg. "It hurts," I said. He knelt before me and took my calf in his farmer's hands, moved up and down, like he was milking. Not looking at me, but watching my skin uddered beneath his fingers.

Over his shoulder I saw Jeannie. She pursed her lips, gave me the finger, and put her towel over her head. "Enough, Daddy," she said. "Enough."

3

Jeannie's dad told her she could drive the boat back to the dock. He sat in the seat beside her and I sat behind her and watched the frothy wake we left, watched the shore from the corners of my eyes. I could still feel the warmth of his hands on my calf.

Jeannie stood at the wheel, beeped the horn at other boats, drove too fast, and went faster still when her dad told her to slow down. We passed a boat filled with boys from our school, older boys. Jeannie raised an arm and whoop-whooped at them. They honked and held up their beers.

"Those boys better watch out for sheriff patrol," her dad said.

"Whatever," Jeannie said.

The camp on the backside of the lake had originally belonged to Jeannie's grandfather. We used to spend long stretches of time at the camp with Jeannie's mom before she got sick. She'd pack us in the car with enough Black Velvet & Ginger to last her a week and we'd head out without even saying goodbye to Jeannie's dad. "It's a girls' day," her mom said as she mixed one of her drinks. We were allowed one beer to split as we sat out on the chaise longues by the water. When she was almost finished with her second drink, she'd let us have a cigarette to split. Then she'd say, "Girls, after this drink, let's go to the mall. We'll buy clogs. We'll get our ears pierced."

I would say yes, yes and Jeannie would say, "Don't be stupid, Mom."

I wanted Jeannie's mom to say that I could stay with them forever. But she'd always bring me home, back to the house where Poppy and I used to live before he died and Aunt May came to take care of me. Then Jeannie's mom got sick and never went back to camp.

Jeannie drove the boat fast up to the dock and pulled back just as we were almost there. Her dad said, "Whoa." Jeannie laughed.

Her dad and I reached out, grabbed the dock, and scrambled out to tie the boat up on either end. We did not look at each other.

Jeannie wrapped her towel over her shoulders and jumped out next to me. "Come on, Paula," she said and tugged my arm, lifting me to my feet. "Let's go get a beer." She grabbed my hand and pulled me past her dad. My leg brushed the crackly golden hair on his arm. I lowered my eyes to him as I passed. He looked hollow. A chocolate Easter bunny, detailed on the outside, and inside, full of air, empty. I wanted to bite through his skin and see what was underneath.

4

By the time we were back for a new school year, Jeannie's mother was dying. In the bright lights of the cafeteria, Jeannie told me she hoped it would happen soon. That her mother would die. "Is it because of the pain?" I said.

She waved a hand at me. Shook her head. There was no pain anymore. "Cheering tryouts are week after next," Jeannie said. "Don't want her to screw them up for me."

Then she drank the rest of her Diet Rite and left me sitting there, thinking about how sweet the breath smells the next morning. That sweet breath of the drinker, fat blackberries, hot from the sun, and hemlock in the spring when the branches finger out with fresh green needles.

I thought of Jeannie's mother in her hospital room, a catheter catching her piss, not having to worry anymore if she said something shameful. Just letting herself sit in clean white sheets, drinking and dying.

I remembered her sweet breath as she leaned over me one sunny afternoon and said, "We will get clogs one of these days, Paula." The air from her mouth tickled me. "Just you and me."

5

Come spring, Jeannie's mother was gone. One day she was alive and sneaking drinks from her sippy cup filled with Black Velvet and water and the next she was dead.

At the funeral, Jeannie didn't cry. I sat next to her in the pew and let the tears come gentle from my eyes. I blew my nose with the Kleenex Aunt May had given me and offered Jeannie some but she just sat there, staring forward. Afterwards, when I gave her a hug and asked her if she wanted to do something—like go to her camp or something and just sit and be quiet, just be like we used to do, when we could dangle our feet over the edge of the dock and listen for the loons—Jeannie said, "Don't be stupid" and walked away, leaving me standing by the car with her dad.

He said, "Don't take it personal, Paula. She's hurting." I didn't look at him, just nodded. Then he snuffled in his snot and I realized he was crying.

I put my arm around him as I'd seen others do on television when faced with grieving. I said, "There, there. There, there."

He asked, "Come with me?" My arm felt heavy along his back, a yoke that he would pull. We got in his truck. When we passed through the four corners, I saw Jeannie out in front of the teen center with a group of boys, older ones. They were all laughing, and so was Jeannie but her lips were tight across her teeth. It was the face she made when she was trying not to cry.

Jeannie's dad bought a six-pack at the Chevron and we drove around drinking it. It was one of those early spring days when you feel like maybe this time summer's going to fool you and come on quick and hot. The air was thick and the light was buttery, like June light, but it was only May. He showed me all the places he used to park with his wife back before she was his wife. Back when they were my age and dating. "Hot and heavy," he said. "We sure were." He smiled thinking about it. "She was a looker, that one. I remember the first time I saw her on her Daddy's farm. She was out haying in her brassiere and cut offs. Built like a brick shit house, that one." He took a swig from his beer and turned the corner down the road that led to their house. "You remind me of her. The way she was back then."

I took a drink from my beer to cover my lack of words. It felt good and bad to be there with him in the truck, like we were dating or like he was my dad telling me stories about my dead mom. It felt like that.

He pulled the truck into the driveway, stopped it, leaned over the steering wheel and drained his beer, turned his head to me and said, "We're out of beers. Let's go in and get some more."

I shrugged. Said, "Okay." But it didn't feel okay. The light was heavy now, casting judgment upon me.

He got out of the truck and came around and opened my door, held his hand out to me and helped me down. He kept holding my hand as he brought me into the kitchen and up to the fridge. He opened it and said,

"Let's see." He bent down and pulled out a couple of beers, held them in his free hand by their necks and took my arm and nudged it behind my back, as he pushed into me so that I was up against the counter. He set the beers down and leaned into me, pressing hot thighs against me.

He lifted his free hand up to my face and touched me on the cheek with two rough fingers. "Do you know what it means to be pretty, Paula?" It was such an odd question that I almost laughed but I was scared what he would do. His breath was hotter and closer and my face felt steamed. I wondered if I should protect myself. Fight or play dead or something. Then he was kissing me, using the same tongue his daughter had used. Tickling my teeth, pushing, pushing into me and moaning. I moved my knee between his legs. I thought I might bring it up swiftly into his groin, to fight back, but I didn't.

His hands grabbed the back of my head and pushed my mouth harder onto his as though he would eat my face; pull it right from the bone. His hands moved inside my skirt and down into my underpants. I was embarrassed that he could feel me down there. Touch my tender skin with his hard fingers.

I felt that the moment might linger like that, hold us in its arms, protect us from each other. I wanted it to go no further or to never stop.

The door swung open on its hinges, then. His hand slipped away.

It was Julius. "Hey there," he called out. He'd come to work when Jeannie's mom had gotten worse sick and her dad had to be at the hospital more. He told Jeannie he was saving up for when his dad retired. He wanted to run his own farm someday. Jeannie thought he was a hottie and so did I but I never admitted it.

Jeannie's father pushed me away, hard against the counter, wiped his mouth, moved to the sink, where he turned on the tap. "Yeah," he said, "Right here, Son."

Julius walked in and stood there in the kitchen right near me and he must have known. He must have seen us through the window in the door. I looked at the ground.

Jeannie's dad kept his back turned and busied himself with wiping up around the sink with a sponge.

"Done milking," Julius said. "Thought I'd come and see if there's anything else I can do to help."

Jeannie's dad said, "If you could bring this girl home, I'd appreciate it. She's come looking for Jeannie and Jeannie's not here."

Like that, I was this girl. So much nothing.

"Meet you out front?" Julius said to me and I nodded without looking up.

Jeannie's dad pulled me over to him, breathed into my hair, kissed me. "You be a good girl," he said.

6

On the ride home, Julius told me about cows. About how everyone thinks they're stupid animals but not him. He thinks they're kind and generous and that they give of themselves freely so that we might feed our children. "They know how to love," he said. "They know that love is all about sacrifice." And the way his face looked in profile as I sat beside him in his pickup, and the way he smelled of hay and manure but it smelled so sweet, and the way his voice was soft and not pleading—those ways are what told me that he and I would not end here.

I felt that maybe I could clean the feeling of Jeannie's dad's lips off my face. Then Julius turned to me and I thought about how up on Poppy's mountain, there was already a red tinge to the trees, leaves getting ready to unfurl.

MERCY

This island had seen its day. The hotel walls tiled in turquoise at one time matched the ocean, now brown and frothy from winter storms. The grout in the swimming pool had rusted and there were often leaves and palm fronds at the bottom. Early one morning, Lizzie watched the pool cleaner lift a small animal from its waters. The soft brown body was turgid, lifeless.

Their hotel was not on the beach; rather it was on the harbor side, so they had to walk to the beach. It took four minutes. They could walk right out a sliding glass door on their room as promised but not onto sand, rather rough grass and a cement sidewalk, which often had amusing lizards on it.

It was not like the island that their mother brought them to after their father died. On that trip, the night before they left, thoughts of her first plane ride kept Lizzie from sleeping, so her mother let her lie on the pullout couch and stay up late. On the plane, her mother gave her a sip of her wine to calm her nerves and when asked how she felt Lizzie said, "I feel edgy."

On that trip, they stayed in a hotel with a newly opened Playboy casino and Lizzie had seen the bunnies in outfits like bathing suits, except with stockings and high heels and ears on their heads.

It was all very *joie de vivre* at that hotel. She'd even been allowed to play a slot machine and the restaurant had blueberry pancakes, which she enjoyed every morning for breakfast. One night it had been just her and Mercy for dinner, their mother otherwise occupied, and when Lizzie ordered custard for dessert and then didn't want to finish it, Mercy made her.

"Small bites," Mercy said. "Don't waste." But the custard stuck on the way down, choking her. And then she thought of her father, and how when they cleaned out his apartment she'd found his calendar of scenic spots and the days when he would see Lizzie and Mercy marked off with a star. And when she remembered the small, green beanbag frog found on his bedside table, her eyes watered. "Don't be a baby," Mercy said and grabbed the custard and ate the rest of it in two bites.

Then when they got back to the room, Mercy went out, leaving Lizzie to read, again, the only book she'd brought, *Black Beauty*. Mercy went to find those two boys from Texas she'd met on the beach. Those teenagers. Lizzie wanted to tell on her but there was no one to tell.

*

Nights were often chilly on this island so they found themselves in jeans just before sunset as their mother and stepfather enjoyed cocktail hour. Their mother was laughing in that way that they hated, so Mercy said they would go to the beach. Lizzie didn't want to go but Mercy looked at her in that way that said I will kill you and so there was no choice.

The sky was thick and low and brownish gray. The clouds like wings of giant jungle birds floating down. Lizzie noticed that with her new perm she was almost as tall as Mercy. She still liked her hair, liked the way it felt spongy on her head, like she was a new person, born into a new family. She was happy with it even though Mercy made fun of it when their mother brought her home from the Hair Nook. "You look like a poodle. A yappy wittle dog. Arf. Arf," Mercy said and held her hands up under her chin like begging paws and stuck out her tongue and pretended to pant. And then she howled louder and louder until Lizzie cried.

Which is what their mother always said Mercy wanted. To make her cry.

At the road, Mercy made her wait and look both ways before they crossed to the beach. It was stupid that she did that. There were no cars. Ever. Only taxis bringing people to their hotel and even those were few and far between.

There was one man on the slippery sand. He had a kite. He might have been young enough to be a teenager except he was not. He pretended not to see them. Mercy said, "I'm going to talk to him."

Lizzie dropped to her knees on the beach, more in a sense of exhaustion than drama, then let her calves fall to the side and her bottom to the sand. It felt cold and not like beach sand should; it should burn your feet, hold the sun. On the other island, the days had been so warm that she'd had to get out of the sun and eat ice cream, which had been watery, chalky. Ice milk is what her mother called it. There was nothing like that on this island.

Mercy stood near the man with a hand up over her eyes, watching the kite and talking, smiling. He turned to her and handed her the kite, then wrapped his arms around her from behind. It was like a hug but not really because he was helping her move the string this way or that. Sometimes they moved their feet in unison, as though they were dancing.

Lizzie watched the kite. It was a bird, wings v-ing out from its body. Its face a hook.

The kite zigged across the sky, moving fast. Mercy and the man walked backwards, pulling the string with them. The wind picked up and the kite billowed upwards and then took a quick dive down, plummeting. Mercy stepped forward, away from the arms around her, but her hair clung to the man's shirt with static, tethering them, so gently.

ORANGE CRUSH

Carrie and I bring hotdog buns and a plastic bottle of vodka to Jay's Fourth of July party. We were supposed to bring hotdogs but I didn't feel like going all the way to the IGA to get them. Jay is drunk already when we get there. "I've been up all night," he says. There are a bunch of guys there we sort of know but they're mostly older, friends of Jay's older brother, Laird.

"Girls, you need a drink." Jay grabs our vodka and takes my hand. Carrie follows. In the kitchen, he mixes vodka and Orange Crush in some plastic cups for us. "Drink up. There's more where that came from."

Carrie always drinks slowly but I don't. I rush everything. I gobble, I gulp, but luckily I'm skinny. Carrie is slow because she worries all the time. I tell her she needs to live a little, but she'd rather be a baby still. I'm so over her.

"Drink up, Care Bear," Jay says and pokes Carrie in her belly where a roll of fat sticks out over her low riders. Same old story: he teases her and she giggles. She won't say it out loud but I know she likes Jay. Jay has liked me since we were little kids. We would play in the sand with our bottles filled with apple juice while our moms drank wine on ice in their chaise lounges.

The lawn, covered in patches of brown where Jay's dog has peed on it, slopes down to the sandy beach and lake below us. Laird and his friends are trying to roll down the hill in an inner tube. The aim is to not fall out until you hit the water. Not one of them has made it all the way yet.

"Hey Jules." Laird motions me over. "Get your skinny butt in here." All of Laird's friends look at me.

"Do you see them checking me out?" I whisper to Carrie. "Nuh uh," I say to Laird and shake my head.

"C'mon," Laird says. "Worried your hair will get messed up?"

"I didn't bring my suit." I hook my thumbs into my belt loops

"So?" He's smiling at me now, letting me know what will happen if I don't do what he wants: he'll ignore me later, pretend that he doesn't even know I exist. I hand Carrie my cup and unzip my pants.

"Julie," Carrie says. "What're you doing?"

"Going in the tube." I slide my pants down my legs and drape them over Carrie's arm. I pull my tank top up over my head and put that on her arm too. She doesn't move or say anything but I think it's funny so I laugh.

"Lighten up," I say. "Jesus fucking Christ, will you lighten up?" I stand before them all in my black boy briefs and bra. Jay coughs and goes into the house. I point to the tube and say, "Give me that thing."

*

Laird and I sit on the lawn under a tree and play crazy eights. I win game after game and then Laird gets bored or tired of losing more likely and lies down on his back.

"Come," he says and motions me into the crook of his arm. I lie next to him and put my hand on his naked chest. The leaves above us are swaying and clinging to the light. The sun finds its way in every once in a while and lightens a spot on my face. I feel warm and Laird's skin is velvet and lamb's ears. His skin is butter and chocolate. I consider rubbing my tongue across his nipple because I think he'd like that. I move my head up a bit, thinking I might kiss him.

"What's your friend's name?" Laird has his hand over his eyes.

"Carrie?" I say.

"She's cute," he says.

"You think?" I put my head back down. "She's kind of fat." I feel like biting his nipple off, like drowning Carrie in the lake.

"Nah," he says. "That's just baby fat. She'll grow out of it."

I move onto my side.

"She's got a nice rack," he says.

I sit up.

"Hey." Laird grabs the back of my shirt and pulls. "You jealous or something?" He laughs.

"Of her? No." I laugh. "No way."

"I'm not done with you yet," he says. I lie there as he falls asleep. I think about how much I hate Carrie.

*

When I wake up later, Laird is gone. He has left me lying alone beneath the tree. My mouth feels dry and filled with poison and I need to pee. I head up to the house and see Jay and Carrie sitting at the picnic table talking. Before they see me I hear Carrie saying something about "she" and "her." I know for a fact she's talking about me. They are always talking about me.

In the bathroom mirror, I catch a glimpse of my mother in the mirror, but it's actually me. I wad up some toilet paper and hold it on the cold water then I dab it on my face, under my eyes and I look fourteen again, blonde hair smooth and parted in the middle, my teeth white and not stained like Mommy's, my skin unwrinkled. I think, "I am not old. I am young."

I go find Jay and Carrie. They are still in the same spot but when they see me they stop talking. "Hey bitches," I say and sit down next to Jay and give him a nibble on his earlobe. He flinches. So does Carrie.

"Cut it out, Jules." Jay pushes me away.

"Sorr-ee," I say but I'm pissed.

"It's okay. It just hurt." He's lying. Carrie smiles at him.

"So what are you guys talking about?" I look right at her.

"Nothing," Carrie says, "Just books and stuff."

"Oh." I yawn. "Can I bum a smoke?"

Carrie digs around in her ugly, ratty bag and slides her pack of cigarettes over to me. I pick them up and walk away.

"Hey," she whines after me.

"Don't have a cow," I say. "I'll bring them back."

I sit on the dock and put my feet in. It's still early in the afternoon and there are hours before fireworks. I wonder if I should ask Jay if he wants to go for a walk. I look back up to the picnic table where he and Carrie are laughing.

I jump into the water with my clothes on and stare up at the sky. All I can hear is the water breathing in and out of my ears.

I might just stay like this for the rest of the day.

*

I am lying in the sun, in my underwear on the dock. Carrie is standing over me. She has a plastic cup in each hand. "What?" I say.

She sits down next to me and hands me a cup. "Thought you might want a drink."

"Oh, thanks." I take it and lift my head to drink half of it in one gulp. The orange tickles the roof of my mouth, the vodka burns. I put my head back down and swallow. "Thanks."

"Are you having fun?" she asks and looks off across the water.

"I guess." I close my eyes and let the sun take me.

"I am," she says, "having fun."

"Good for you." I roll onto my stomach.

"Can I tell you something?" she asks and I shrug. "I sort of like Jay."

"No duh!" I say.

"You knew?"

"Who doesn't know? You're so, like, blatant about it."

"Oh," she says, blushes, takes a sip of her drink.

"Don't get all embarrassed," I say.

"I'm not," she says, but she has a pout on. "Can I ask you something?"

"What?" I hate it when people ask if they can ask. Just ask.

"Do you think he likes me?" She won't look at me for my answer.

There are so many things I could say but I don't. I shrug again.

"Really, Julie. Do you?" Now she's looking at me and there's something sad about the way she's begging me to say yes.

"No," I say and roll off the dock into the water. I stay under as long as I can, holding my breath. Above me I see Carrie crying, her nice rack heaving. I let out air bubbles when I laugh. She doesn't seem to notice.

*

"Where are the fucking dogs, man!" Laird is yelling at Jay, who is standing there like a dumb ass.

"Julie was supposed to bring them," Jay says and they both look at me.

"There weren't any at the IGA," I lie.

"There were no hot dogs? On July Fourth? None?" Laird waves a spatula around like a wand.

"Nope," I say. "None."

"Well, this is totally going to suck," he says.

"We still have burgers," Jay says.

"Nah, we need dogs, man. Dogs!" Laird's face is getting red. "You brats need to go find some. Go somewhere else to look."

Jay looks at me. "C'mon Julie. Let's go."

"I'm not going," I say. "Ask Carrie to go."

"She left," he says.

"What?" I have a hard time not smiling.

"She went home," Jay says and looks back over his shoulder. "You were swimming. She said she didn't feel well."

"All right," I say, "I'll go get stupid hot dogs with you."

"Hurry back, kiddies," Laird says and waves to us with the spatula. Behind him his friends are playing a fucked up game of bocce on the lawn. One of them is trying to juggle and another one whisks a tiny broom behind his ball as it scoots across the grass.

I look where Carrie and I left our bikes and hers is missing. Jay and I get in Laird's truck. Jay doesn't even have his permit yet but Laird lets him drive all the time. I climb in the passenger side; it feels familiar that I should be there, close, like sitting on the couch with Jay and playing video games. I turn on the radio and sing loud. I bounce up and down on the seat and sing louder. Jay drives in silence. I turn off the radio.

I say, "Where're we going?"

"Baxter's," he says.

"That's like 15 miles away. It'll take forever."

I slide over closer to him on the seat and put my hand on his thigh. He flinches a bit. I rub his leg and then kiss his neck. "Quit fooling around, Jules," he says. "I'm trying to drive."

"Whatever," I say.

"I just want to get the stupid hot dogs," he says. We're on a dirt road with our windows down and outside dust is flying up as high as the windows and over, blotting out the corn, not yet high enough, in the fields

The words have been hanging there so long, waiting. I have to get them out of my mouth. "Are you in love with Carrie or something?"

"No," he says, too quickly. "She's cute. I like her."

"What do you mean cute?" I know for a fact that she's not prettier than I am.

"She's pretty. Got a pretty face," he says and his eyes are forward out the window, squinting, not looking at me, seeing something else.

"And a nice rack." I say, crossing my arms over my chest and slamming back against the seat.

"You're so rude," Jay says.

"Laird likes her tits." Jay hates it when I mention Laird. Ever since Laird and I first hooked up when our families were together last Christmas Eve, Jay's been pissed. We're not even going out or anything. As Laird says, "We're friends with benefits."

"Yeah, well Laird likes a lot of things." Jay's face is cold and hard, the lake frozen over.

"Laird likes me," I say.

"Yeah, sure he does," Jay says.

"What? He does like me. I know for a fact he likes me," I say, not so sure that it's true.

*

There are other girls at the party when we return. Older girls. "Here come the dogs!" Laird yells when he sees us and a girl next to him swats his ass.

"Don't call her that! She's cute," the girl says.

"I wasn't talking about Jules. I was talking about the hot dogs. I know that Jules is cute, but not as cute as you, baby." He grabs the girl and kisses her and I feel my belly tighten up, my thighs clench. Laird stops kissing her and waves me over. "Bring the dogs, kiddo." He turns around and I throw the hot dogs at him so that they hit him one, two on the back.

Then I run. I pick up the inner tube and I run with it and I get myself inside and roll it all the way down to the lake. I hear Jay calling my name but I don't stop. I roll until there is no more grass, just me and water.

"What's wrong with you, Jules?" Jay says as he looks for a sweatshirt I can borrow among his things. The sun has gone down and I'm cold. "Why are you acting so crazy today?"

"I don't know," I say. Jay has a plush blanket on his bed with a wolf design . He's had it since we were about ten. We used to lie under it together and pull it over our heads and tell stories and sometimes we would get undressed to our underwear and look at each other, or touch each other.

"Here," Jay hands me a hoodie and then goes to leave.

"Wait," I say, grabbing his arm. His skin feels warm under my cool, blue-tinged fingers. "Lie under the blanket with me for a second so I can warm up?" He looks at me.

"Okay," he says. "But just for a second."

He gets underneath the blanket and I stand on his rug, dripping. I pull the arm of my tank top over my head.

"What are you doing?" Jay tries to get out of the bed but I push him back down.

"I'm getting naked. Close your eyes if you don't like it." He closes his eyes and covers them with his hand. Naked, I crawl under the covers and snuggle against his rigid body. When he puts his warm hand against my cold back, I look up at him and his face is red.

I kiss him on his lips, which soft and open and I feel that they might be what love is—warm, wet.

"Quit fooling around, Jules," Jay says, pushing me away.

"I'm not." I try to kiss him again.

"No," he says. "I don't want you to kiss me."

I sit up and the blanket falls away from me. He can see me naked on the top now. I smile at him and he tries to cover me back up.

"I don't want this," he says, looking young, looking like he did when we were ten.

"Why not?" I know for a fact that he does want this—me naked here with him—has always wanted it.

"Because I don't," Jay says and crawls over me. He leaves the room and the screen door slams behind him as he goes outside. I pull the wolf blanket over my head and wait for someone to come get me.

*

I leave the house when I hear the fireworks and everyone cheering. I take Jay's sweatshirt with me because the smell of it reminds me of something, safe and happy. Outside, I see Carrie's bike is back against another tree and that she and Jay are sitting on the picnic table holding hands. Laird is standing on the lawn with a girl on either side of him.

I get on my bike and pedal away as fast as I can. Above me the sky lights up again and again with the fireworks from the summer camp. Each light is like that feeling of a guy's hand on you when he really likes you. That feeling of warmth and crushing bones, of skin licking skin and teeth clanging teeth. Each time the sky lights with red or blue, I feel it and I ride my bike faster.

I ride until I can't breathe or see the sky anymore. I ride until everything is just a blur.

CELESTIAL

Moira rode her bike like a six-year-old: pedal, pedal, pedal, coast. Pedal, pedal, pedal, coast. A cigarette dangled from her lips as she wove in and out of traffic. Passing the dark splotch on the tar just past the Quik Mart, she discreetly signed the cross. That splotch was all that remained of some guy whose head had been run over by a city bus when his bike veered into traffic. Apparently the head had squished, or, more appropriately, popped like a big juicy melon. He was wearing a helmet. She never did.

This is what she did every day: ride her bike all the way to work, and then she would bring it into the store. It would be safe there in the basement with all the other bikes. But fuck that. It was a stolen bike anyway. She didn't steal it but the guy she bought it from—Jason, the ex-pro roller-figure-skater—probably did. It was only $50 but it was a nice mountain bike, electric blue. She put stickers on it in case the owner was one of those kids she tried to hit at BU, where she aimed for the people in the crosswalk instead of avoiding them.

It was precarious. Always. The ride.

Case in point: the night before something had happened. Something she couldn't quite put into words or form thoughts around. It was an instant that left her feeling as though she were longing for something or someone. She felt missing.

After closing the store and counting the cash in the back room with Jeppy—who wanted to be an actor but had stringy hair and crossed eyes and a stumpy girlfriend with a shelf of an ass—she had gotten on her bike and headed home, just like always. She was tired after hours of standing on a concrete floor, under fluorescent tubes with music screeching, video screens flashing. Her brain felt crusted over with images and talking and money changing hands. As she approached that large building just before the slight rise and one of the bridges leading nowhere, she saw a guy walking, flicking in and out of the lamplight, across the cement field leading up to the street and a waiting cab.

It seemed one of those moments of random crossings. She would likely pass the cab, just as he was sitting down in the plush seat, breathing in the air freshener, listening to the static on the radio. Those moments were not to be ignored. They could mean the difference between a melon and a head.

Once she had picked up a piece of paper someone had dropped and handed it to the person, meeting eyes, eyes meeting. And then he went one way and she went another. It might have easily ended differently. She might have gone home with the guy and found out that he liked to keep girls in a cage in his basement. She might still be there, wearing a neon green T-shirt and singing karaoke with him when he came home at night, drunk, breath smelling sour of bathroom blowjobs. He would videotape the two of them and it would look like they were having fun but then when the tapes surfaced and played on "Inside Edition," it would be clear that the setting was an unfinished space, the walls fruitlessly stuccoed into a dusty meringue. Singing "Karma Chameleon," Moira would smile listlessly for the camera.

Or the time she was pumping up her bike tires and the guy in the fucking Mercedes asked her if she partied and she shook her head no. But she might have said yes and gotten in his car and she might have been the one they found one hot summer morning in the dumpster. Headless. Her naked torso without hands or face, her skin pale against the rusty metal. Metal rusting.

It was a chance. A random crossing.

So the guy was walking out to his cab and Moira approached on her bike, in the dark, pedaling slowly, her hands loose on the handles, as he opened the door to the cab. And when she was 100 feet away, a voice: "No. No. No." And feet slapping on pavement. A man, thin and pale and clothes-less, ran to the cab-entering-man and hugged him from behind. "You can't leave," the naked man said. "No." She turned her head as she passed, catching the embrace, keeping it. She was pedaling harder then, up hill and looking back over her right shoulder. She saw the headlights of the cab and the dark blob of bodies and then nothing as she crested the hill and descended.

Then she coasted, heavy with never having wanted that much.

But to be on the streets alone like that. Late at night. With her feet humming and her fingers still moving from counting money. To be out and breathing in the chocolate air.

When she got home, Moira didn't go right to bed like she should have. Instead, her stolen bike safely tucked in the alcove at the top of the stairs, she went out onto the porch and pulled down the ladder which led to the roof, climbed it and pushing off the lid, she entered the silent expanse of flat tar, warm from the late setting sun. Up there was all nascent stillness with the chance of stars cutting through the ambient light, surprising as they sliced through the dark.

LIAR

Lisa's room was small but artful and Cassie coveted it. Her own room seemed that of a young girl still—the walls papered in images of red and pink giraffes and elephants, were thumb-tacked with posters of her heroes—William Shatner and Leonard Nimoy—yellowed and peeling at the edges from age. Her bed was a mess of stuffed animals and the floor a wasteland of rumpled clothing.

The floor of Lisa's room was pale blue shag and the walls, a fine faux wood panel upon which hung matted and framed drawings and sketches from Lisa's own hand. The lake at sunset. Their mother's face in profile. An oak tree. A study of their dead father as a child—wearing a large hat, riding a white horse.

Cassie thought the pictures were nice, though they seemed hollow to her. As though their bones were exposed, their hearts beating too wildly through chalky ribs. They seemed, somehow, desperate. But the teachers said that Lisa was gifted in art and she was supposed to be going to art school but she had not gotten enough aid and so worked at their stepfather's five-and-dime store instead. Her plan was to save money, keep working on her art, and apply again in a year.

"I'm going to get out of here, Cassie," is what she said, sitting on the shag, back leaning up against the box spring. "They won't keep me here."

And Cassie had nodded and cajoled. Agreed with her sister that, yes, she would escape and become an artist in New York City. But Cassie was secretly glad that her sister was kept back. Glad that she would not be going away. Cassie had feared being the one left behind to watch and listen to their mother and stepfather as they talked and ate with the air singing out their noses, lips smacking, juice gathering in their gullets. Had feared being the one left to hear her mother call out her stepfather's name in the night behind their closed door.

After dinner, they would sit together in Lisa's room and play Tom Petty or Bruce Springsteen over and over. Or they'd put on something older—something that would make them sad, like Cat Stevens and think about their father but not talk about him.

Instead they would talk about how things were with Lisa and her boyfriend, Scott. Recently, Lisa had admitted that Scott told her that she was very good at something. Very good. And then she had whispered, "Sex." They had never used that word before—together, like that, as sisters. Cassie was embarrassed, titillated.

Her sister was good at sex.

Scott liked it when she was on top, Lisa said. He liked it when she reached her hand around and held his balls in her hand. He liked to put his penis between her breasts.

Cassie tried to picture these scenarios—her sister, hair wild and loose, straddling Scott, the farm boy. But all she could see was herself. Her hand reaching for Scott's balls. Her breasts enfolding his penis.

Cassie and Scott had never talked much but she had known the sound of his mouth for years—his mouth on her sister's mouth as they made out on the couch on Saturday nights while she sat in the Barcalounger trying to watch television. Often Cassie would hear him moan as he smacked lips with her sister. On those nights she could not wait for him to go and for it to be a cool, crisp Sunday morning when she could get up alone, untethered. She would make Pop Tarts, which she would eat while watching reruns of *Star Trek*.

"He thinks you're cute," Lisa said and got up to flip the record. "Real cute." Cassie blushed then, not wanting to admit that she knew for a fact that Scott thought so. He had smiled at her once. Looked her up and down and nodded. They looked very much alike, after all, she and her sister. Except Cassie was taller, lankier, less womanly, which both worried and pleased her.

Cassie had never had a boyfriend like Lisa had. Only boys whose cars she had taken rides in on cold winter nights. Only Mr. Whiting her Chemistry and then Physics teacher whose dick she often sucked in the room behind the lab after school. He had once asked her to take her clothes off just so he could look at her. She stripped to her underwear and stood sock-footed on the cool Terrazzo tile with her back to the crusty beakers and large, soapstone sinks, as he examined her. "You are pretty," he said. "A pretty girl."

Cassie justified these moments by telling herself that Mr. Whiting was more like a friend than a teacher. He was into the same stuff she was, like *Star Trek* and the new *Twilight Zone* movie that was being made. They had mourned together when the helicopter crashed on set, killing the star of the movie.

"It may be the biggest tragedy of our times," Mr. Whiting had said to her as they stood side-by-side and read the newspaper account. Cassie had nodded. Yes. She was his lab assistant for extra credit. It had seemed a great item to add to her college applications. That's how he pitched it to her anyway, "You know how hard it is for girls in science? Well, this will give you that extra edge, Cass."

And she had been grateful but not so grateful that she went to the back room easily. It had taken some work at first, "Come on, Cass," Mr. Whiting said, index fingers tucked in his pockets, "I won't hurt you." But then, after that first time, his cool penis in her warm mouth, his hand on her head, caressing and pushing down, it had gotten easier. She'd grown to like it. It made her feel special. She felt an alien on a strange planet. One that James T. Kirk would find and fall in love with.

*

The temperature had dropped overnight from the low forties to thirties. It was snow weather and a few flakes were swirling along the sidewalk in front of the IGA.

Ever since they banned cigarettes in the grocery store, their mother refused to go shopping anymore. If Cassie and Lisa wanted to eat, she said, it was up to them to get the food. They were shopping not just for regular food but for food for the annual Christmas Eve party their mother and stepfather held every year at their house for the five-and-dime employees. Lisa led the way and Cassie followed behind with the cart. The aisles were jammed with mothers and children, free from school for the holiday.

Cassie wanted to get a few bags of chips and call it a day. "These people are such scrounges anyway," she said. But Lisa was insistent on her menu: clam chowder, mincemeat pie, and pigs in blankets. Cassie had a feeling it was because Martin was going to be there.

He was new to the five-and-dime, hired in for the holidays, and Cassie had hoped that maybe he wouldn't be there but she knew he would. He was older, in his twenties, and had a mustache that made him, Cassie thought, look like an impostor. She had never known what he looked like without it, but it seemed to be hiding something about him. Her mother called him a flirt. He flirted with the female customers. He flirted with Cassie. And, especially, he flirted with Lisa when she worked her shift. Cassie had taken to making faces behind his back whenever she saw him.

A bearded man in a stained T-shirt started following them in Baking supplies. Whenever Lisa stopped to reach for something on the shelves, he would stop as well, pick up a box or a bag and read the ingredients. In Canned Goods, when Lisa had crouched down to grab some soup, he stooped next to her, flipped open a penknife and sliced a thread from the bottom of her sweater. Lisa froze until he held the thread up to her, offered it to her like a gift.

No one had ever done that for Cassie.

*

The party had been going for an hour and Cassie had already had two glasses of wine. It was packed not only with people who worked at the five-and-dime now but past employees as well. "Don't these people have homes?" she whispered to Lisa as they filled the chip bowls. "I mean, you'd think they'd want to be with their families or something."

"Don't be such a brat," Lisa said and tucked her hair behind her ears. Cold air from the open front door swept down the hallway as Martin entered the party. Lisa's expression changed from placid to delighted as he shook off his peacoat and headed towards them.

Cassie moved away, then, not wanting to hear his voice and watched them from a distance. Lisa and Martin, mixing drinks at the breakfast nook and then laughing over a bowl of pretzels at the butcher block. She'd seen Scott standing alone, watching them, too. Seen his eyes skim up and down Lisa, as though she were a Ford F-150 he coveted. His face in that moment looked just like their stepfather's had when he pinched Cassie's nub of a breast at age 12 and said her mother ought to get her a bra. The eyes were black and thoughtless, like a dead animal, like a bird about to peck the dead eyes out of a dead, dead animal.

She understood his unhappiness, his anger, as he watched Lisa with Martin. She felt it herself. Lisa shouldn't be laughing with Martin; Lisa belonged to them.

Cassie wanted to somehow get Scott this message—telepathically. To pinch him in the neck the way Spock would and let him know what she was thinking. He turned to her. Met her eyes—his gray to her blue and smiled. It seemed like it would be a nice smile, to an outsider.

Then he was before her, without her realizing that enough time had passed for him to make the trip across the room. Perhaps the transporter had been utilized, breaking him down to his molecules and shuttling him across the room.

"Let's go smoke," he whispered in her ear, a hand on her elbow. She'd never smoked with him without Lisa before. She'd had her first joint with Lisa when she was twelve and had done her first line of coke with Lisa and Scott, in the backseat of his Monte Carlo the year prior. It felt wicked and so she wanted to do it. To show Lisa that she and Scott could have something private, too, like buddies, like people who loved her and were pissed off.

Cassie looked to where Lisa was leaning against the breakfast nook, Martin practically spooning her from the side, and realized that the warmth she was feeling was Scott's hot breath in her ear.

The hair on her arms was on fire. The wine made her feel godless and elated. This gone-right-to-the-headness had never happened before in the history of wine. Never happened in the history of Cassie. Never, in fact, happened in the history of Cassie and wine as a collective. Never.

"Okay," she said and followed him out.

Outside, below the stairs that led up to their house, an apartment above the store, Scott leaned his tall body into her and opened his wide, warm mouth onto hers. She felt those same smacking lips, smacking but this time it felt different. His tongue inside her mouth was a soft animal. Not so unlike Mr. Whiting's penis, lying there and waiting for her to act, to bring it to life.

It was her own kiss. Too big and too generous. Not what she had expected. All of the boys who had taken her in their cars and behind buildings had been tense, terse with their mouths or too sloppy and greedy. But this kiss, this kiss was love and it was not meant for her but it was the most pure kiss. Because it was not just Scott kissing her but about the three of them kissing together, binding her to her sister, perfectly.

It was the kiss of a brother to a sister, to a sister, nothing more. It was a long gulp of wine burning down her throat. Until she realized it was all about giving back, getting even and then she moved into it and then pushed away, her hands on his chest. And when they went back up the stairs to the party, no one had realized they were gone, Lisa still frozen in the same laugh she had been. Martin still attached to her side.

It wasn't until Lisa had left Martin to go to the bathroom that Cassie had a chance to say anything. She crowded in behind her sister.

"Hey," Lisa said, pushing against Cassie. "Wait your turn, kid."

It was something about "kid." Something about the way it rolled off Lisa's tongue so easily, pushing Cassie back and away. She felt something, then, moving across her back and into her armpits. It was that feeling she had in class sometimes when she knew the right answer and she knew that she knew but wasn't sure whether she should raise her hand or not or whether she would have the opportunity to be called upon and to then say what she knew and receive the praise she deserved.

Cassie said, "He kissed me."

"Who?" Lisa said. "Santa?"

"Scott kissed me."

Lisa's eyes turned white then. White-gold dead. Cassie felt them slice through her skull and reach down through her neck into her vertebrae, and slink into her heart, stopping it completely. "Are you sure?" is what Lisa said, but Cassie knew she was really saying, "You are a liar."

She pushed out of the room then and out the door, down the stairs. She was vaguely aware of people calling her name. Of Scott. Of Martin. Her mother's soft-voiced, "Babe, where you going?" But she was gone. In the shed, she found her bike, creaky from the cold nights but still serviceable. She jumped on it and veered onto the snow-dusted road. She took her hands off the handles, and coasted down the hill to the lake.

Her sister thought she was a liar.

It was not something Kirk would have ever thought of Spock. And if he did, he never would have let Spock know. There would have been integrity.

SHAME

I should be running along a path after jumping, breathless, from a stony bank into a chasm filled with mossy water and shivery, splintered rocks.

I should be running wet-haired and age thirteen up a path away from the water and the voices calling me. Voices, waiting for girls in cut offs, donning scabbed over bug bites as camouflage. Girls in shirts with iron on decals proclaiming, "Disco is Dead but Rock is Rolling."

My shame should be hard-hearted and smoldering, the whole walk home, tar sticking to the bottoms of sockless sneakers. So hot I should dip my toes into the icy brook from which the cows drink, small fish darting, insidious in the grass.

Later shivering in a sleeping bag on the lawn, all crabgrass and dandelion, I should watch the cold night pass above the hemlocks. Waiting for the dew to wake me, when the scrawny cur with the rotting head of a heifer in its jaws comes home to show me what he has found.

WE
ARE
AWAKE

We were looking for a supermarket but the one I remembered had closed down. The K-Mart was gone, too. My sister and I had bought bathing suits there one year. Not good quality; they did not last the summer.

The dog was in the back of the car, whining because he had diarrhea from the trip. We parked in the middle of the lot and walked him in the tall, yellow grass.

I held back and listened to Jess whisper to the dog, "Good boy. That's right. Good boy."

They often talked like this—without me. Weeds grew up between the cracks in the asphalt.

I remembered that the grocery store had a wall of videotapes on the left when you walked in. I rented *Eraserhead* but fell asleep watching it. Where were the videos now that the store was gone? Where was *Eraserhead*?

*

We are awake, often, in the night. There are noises.

There are owls.

One who sounds like an owl, and one who sounds like your soul slipping past death.

There are screams. Inhuman. Inhumane. Animals killing each other or fucking—it's hard to tell the difference between the two.

And the dog barks and comes to the bed for comfort. We stroke his head and lie there listening.

When you sleep in a tent you hear every whisper of the people in the site next to yours. Every mouse sifting through the fire pit. Every widowmaker in the trees that cracks and falls to the ground.

But in a house, you should hear only the hum of the refrigerator. The furnace ticking on and off. The buzz of your computer.

You should not hear the tall pines moaning in the wind.

*

We swam out to the inner tube that was anchored to one of the moorings. The sun had mostly set, but a sliver of it remained on the edge of the mountains to the west.

The water would have been soupy, the air chill, as we clung to the inner tube. He told me again that no matter where you are on Nova Scotia you are only 15 miles from the ocean.

It is an island.

And we were an island. The two of us out in the lake like that as the sun set and the sky got dark, as the moon rose and the stars came out, as our feet kicked slowly through the water, weeds tangling our feet.

We were an island as the wind calmed and the sound of voices across the lake carried, as the lights came on in camps and cottages, as the last boats made their way in from fishing.

We were an island as I held my mouth to the edge of the water and blew bubbles, hoping that he would know that they were really kisses, making their way through the water to his skin.

STATES OF RESIDENCY

Keene, New York

My grandmother was born on a wooden table, in a dark kitchen, in a blue house, in an apple orchard. When she was seven and complained of a sore throat, the same doctor who birthed her took her tonsils out on that rough-hewn table where she was born, where she ate breakfast, lunch and dinner, where she learned how to read and make piecrust.

Later, her tonsils grew back. Or maybe they were never really gone.

She spent most of her life in that orchard. Rode in between the rows of stubby trees on a gray mare named Billie and learned how to make new branches grow from old ones. It's called grafting. You cut the branches at an angle and you find the right tree to attach them to. The more grafts you make the more apples there are. And if you bind the wood just so, it grows together that way, forever.

I don't remember much about the orchard. It was gone by the time I was five or maybe six. I don't remember much except for the dusty white coating on the apples at harvest time, riding in the back of the wagon and jumping off every so often with a basket ready to pick. I would eat too many of the sour fruit and end up with a sore stomach for days.

I don't remember much but the apples, the stomach and the red swing, out in the tall grass by the white barn with green trim where they kept the rusty tractor, the swing where I sat and wondered about apples and branches and how they grow into each other.

*

I saw a guy's dick for the first time. I was fifteen and it had been snowing all day, then at night it turned from snow to wind. Wind and cold. Layla and I drank vodka from a paper bag down at the four corners, the wind blowing down from Canada. Blowing hard and cold. Blowing the breath of Inuits and seals down, down. Blowing the hard, cold breath of the French down, down from Quebec, Montreal, Huntington. All of it rushing down upon us in our small town, on our four corners. If we thought about it hard enough we could feel all of their breath, rubbing our raw cheeks, pushing up our nostrils and into our lungs, pushing against our own breath coming out pale against icy air.

This guy drove by and asked me if I wanted to hang out. I said sure. I said why not. I said could Layla come. But he said no and she said screw it, she didn't want to anyway.

The skin was all leathery looking and weird. He licked my neck and I liked the way his tongue felt like sparks. Then when I kissed him his lips were soft and his mouth tasted like Bazooka and milk.

Later, after he'd already left me and after I'd grown a bit older, I went with his brother. Not because I wanted to piss him off or anything. I wanted to do it. Their dicks were exactly alike.

I think maybe that it was years later when I was with the brother. I'm not sure. I'm not even sure if I really did it.

Maybe I'm wrong about the timing.

✍ *South Hero, Vermont*

Ben and I bought a house together. He'd just gotten out of the Air Force where he learned how to clean all the tiny parts deep in the belly of a jet. All those parts you would never think about when you see one blaze through the sky above you, up there in the pale sky. Even though he had money to burn, his jet part cleaning skills didn't really serve him well out in the real world but buying a house seemed the right thing to do.

We found an old farmhouse with a crawl space basement and an old chicken coop out back. We could hear the coyotes at the sheep farmer's fence all night long.

I felt like I might be new there. I felt like Ben could see me as this clean girl who cooked for him and washed his underwear and take me for that—the girl who lived in the house with him. The girl he would be with forever.

At night he fell asleep before I did. I would stay up and listen to the barks and yips and listen to the owl that flew by and around in circles, through the trees, over the field and back again. The owl that called to me. I would listen to Ben breathing, soft and low and hope that he would never stop breathing beside me.

*

I got the stomach flu and spent a week on the couch rushing back and forth to the bathroom, alternately shitting and puking, puking and shitting. Ben went to work as a prison guard. He left early and got home late, until he got sick too and I had to take care of him.

It snowed hard for a few days running and even though we were weak, we still had to chop the wood for the fire. He chopped and I carried it in through the bulkhead. When he threw up the noodle soup I made him eat, I had to finish up chopping and loading the wood myself. Ben watched me from indoors, every once in a while his white face blinking at me from the window.

*

In the spring, I planted gladiolas. By summer, they came up tall and proud and peach colored along the wall. Then we whitewashed the house and moved. Later we heard that the folks who rented it were keeping goats in one of the spare bedrooms.

Ben said fuck it and let the house go for taxes.

ᐲ *Troy, New York*

The apartment was small but not so small that you couldn't get away from each other. Neither of us had jobs so we went out to look together but our car broke down. We were in between a bunch of broken-windowed factories and thought we were screwed because the streets around us were quiet, empty. But some guy came along in a small red pickup.

He was maybe forty or younger and seemed like an okay guy. Offered to help us. Called a tow truck for us on his cell phone. Then Ben asked him if he'd take me home. Just me alone with the stranger. I went, no problem. Later, when he dropped me off, he gave me his card.

I still have it.

*

When the furnace guy came to fix a leaky valve, I let him in, no problem. In the basement, he told me I ought to be careful and not let just anyone in. He could see the farmhouse all over me. He could see the apple orchard and grafted branches falling away.

*

Ben got a job working with developmentally disabled adults. They were deaf and blind and mostly retarded. He learned tactile sign language and wiped shit off their asses.

Then he fucked the woman he was working with. She used to be a manicurist, which was the detail that bothered me the most. Her nails plucking at his skin. My hand in hers as she examined my crusty cuticles. Dipping my hand in green liquid, You're soaking in it!

I threw the phone book at him and left.

*

For a while, I lived with different people, on couches, sharing beds. I worked in a diner, an ice cream shop, an office supply store.

I fucked: one guy who had a stutter; one guy who was nineteen; and I sucked a gay guy's dick.

In the bathroom at the karaoke bar, a woman asked me if she could take me on a date. I told her I'd think about it.

*

I was living with a girl I met at my job at the bakery. She didn't have an extra room so I slept on the floor of the walk-in closet and only paid a quarter instead of half of the rent.

When my grandmother died, I didn't know who else to call.

Ben said sure, of course, he'd give me a ride up home.

My aunt put us in the same room to sleep. She said we were living in sin anyway. Might as well just own up to it. She didn't know we were apart and we didn't bother to tell her. I got the bed and Ben slept on the floor.

At night, Ben would kneel beside the bed and pet my head before I fell asleep. Then he would kiss me beside my nose, on my lips, my chin. Then he ran his hand down my body over the covers and then under.

I let Ben put his fingers inside me.

And then we had sex in my car in the driveway of the funeral home. He didn't wear a rubber but I was too drunk to say anything. I hoped that I would never have his baby.

On the way back to Troy Ben told me that he and the manicurist were getting married.

I saw the farmhouse explode and fall to rubble. I saw the coyotes run to the woods with sidelong glances, with tails low. I saw my hands in my lap, clasping and unclasping.

Buffalo, New York

I hooked up with this guy from Chicago. He looked just like Christian Slater but he missed his girlfriend or something so he couldn't get it up. We messed around a few times, humping each other with our underwear on, making each other laugh at stupid jokes.

Then he hooked up with the girl who had a tattoo of a dragon that started on her back and wound its scaly tail around her breast. She took off her shirt and showed me, cupped her breasts so gently, her black hair falling, falling over her face.

I wanted to run my finger along her tattoo, to trace it into her skin and then have her draw it on mine. I wanted us to be mirror images of each other but the two of them left the hotel one night.

For the longest time, I couldn't remember her name. But it was Mercedes. Her name was Mercedes.

Atlanta, Georgia

Malachi was a security guard and he was sexy until he smiled and you saw his two front teeth were sort of fucked up, brown and bucked. We had that in common. My teeth had been crooked in front and bucked since I was ten or eleven. I didn't mind his teeth so much.

I would visit him in his booth and we would touch each other. His hand would slip up underneath my shirt and a finger would dart in and out of my bra onto my nipple, like a dragon's tongue. Then at night we would drink rum and coke and have sex on top of his covers.

When I first met him—at a party full of strangers—he just grabbed me and kissed me. Took me by surprise but I wanted him to do it again.

I wanted everyone to do that. To pull me so close that I became a part of them instantly, grafting us together.

*

At another party, I fell asleep in a chair. I'd been working for two days straight without a minute off but Malachi wanted to go out when I got home. He gave me ephedrine to take but it did not wake me up.

When I did wake up, I saw him on the plaid couch across from me, on top of another girl. She was kissing him, her pale arm dangling off the couch, holding her wire-rimmed glasses in hand. Her fingernails tapered and neat. Mine with hangnails and dirt embedded beneath them.

I couldn't move from the chair so I just let it happen. Couldn't even open my mouth. Didn't even care to. Saw his tongue dart in and out of her mouth, his hand move up under her shirt, his finger flicker, the tongue, the dragon. Heard her gasp. Heard her breathe hard and harder.

The next morning, I was still in the chair, sun lighting up the beer cans on the matted orange carpet, the empty jewel cases, the cigarette packs and plastic cups chewed at the edges. Malachi was gone.

I could have been the last person on Earth. A girl on a nubby chair in a dirty room, awake after everything had died.

*

I met Dooley when I got a job as a hostess at Applebee's. He worked the fryer. He said he needed a roommate so I moved in with him after my cousin got sick of me sleeping on her couch.

One night Dooley and I drank too many margaritas. I got angry at him because he told me I should get braces. He said that I'd be hot if my teeth weren't so fucked up. I wanted to tell him that he didn't know anything. Wanted to tell him that he was fat and stupid and that I would never fuck him.

But I didn't or I couldn't so I took off in my bare feet. We were living somewhere out of a main town and the roads were dark. He didn't even come after me and that made me angrier. I guess he didn't care whether I left or not. I guess it didn't matter. We had no connection.

I walked in some of the ditches in case cars came by. The tall grass whispered back and forth in the breeze and tickled my thighs and I slipped in the wetness a few times. I got scared that there might be things in the frothy ditch water—alligators and snakes and whatever else hangs out in ditches. So I got back on the road. The tar still felt hot on my bare feet even though the sun had been down for hours. It felt sweaty and alive, the tar. It felt like it was sliding beneath me, a new skin.

A car came up beside me and some guy poked his beardy face out and told me to get in. He said he was a cop off duty but he could have been anyone. I got in anyway.

He asked me, Where do you live?

And I said, I can't remember.

My house could have been anywhere. Could've been an apple orchard, a hotel room, the back seat of a car. It could have been a farmhouse or a security shack. My house was somewhere, splitting apart and binding back together.

REMEMBER

A road of dirt and stone led past a dusty-drived, red house on the right. On the left, a barbed fence wrapped carelessly around a brawny tree that pointed to a field of mown hay. A doe stopped in her tracks as she passed over the road, snorted, and moved on through a hole in the fence.

(That winter, we walked through the snowy fields just behind the trees. We followed the fence line and laughed at how far our feet sank. We did not worry about being shot by an orange vested hunter.)

The sheep farmer was quiet and young and he could have been my friend. Though he and I never spoke, I heard the voices of his animals every day and every night. I listened for them. The coy-dogs stayed by his sheep fences and sang us (the farmer, me and you, and the sheep) to sleep at night until we were startled, all of us, by the ringing gunshot followed by the absence of song.

I grew a tall garden of corn and sunflowers and tomatoes and pumpkins and lettuce and cucumbers and radishes all in tidy raised rows. More vegetables than we would ever need. So many that some rotted on the vine. But the garden was patiently weeded each day.

And there were mourning doves that sat on the roof and watched me take in my laundry from the line in that moment that was perfection. You were standing with the hood up on your car. We stopped moving, looked up at the roofline, and waited until the wind picked up. Nothing was ever the same after that.

And there was the sound of the bird in the woods that is only in the woods. HEE hee hee hee, HEE hee hee hee and who are you? And who are you?

And there were the Northern Lights—the Aurora Borealis twice that summer—late and so high in the sky that I almost drove off the road. What is it? What is that?

(They say not to whistle when you see the lights or the spirits will cut off your head and play ball with it.)

The stars and black, black sky, the peepers, and the quiet make me wonder what I am doing here in this land of weed whackers and lawn mowers and engines always engines burning and buzzing and burning and buzzing and making a short life shorter.

But here and now it is spring again.

The daffodils rise, wetted with your blood. They raise their happy faces to the sun and say, here I am. The grass greens and the tulips push their way up and out.

The forsythia is in bloom.

This is what I remember now.

QUARTER

We found a discount grocery store, the kind where you have to pay for bags and where you stick a quarter in the slot to get a cart. You get a quarter back in the end, but it's not necessarily yours. That quarter could belong to anyone, but then it's yours, in your hand, your pocket. Money is tricky.

The discount yogurt I bought was too sweet in its sourness, like vomit and dry breath after a night of blackberry brandy.

*

I left the yogurt behind when we vacated the house. I don't know if anyone ate it or if they simply threw it in the trash, knowing where it came from, how it got there. I like to think of it as a quarter I left behind, wedged into the cart like a prize for the next user.

MACAW

There was this one whose little dog would do a handstand in the corner of the couch when I came back to the third-floor apartment with its pharmacist's bookshelves and claw foot tub—one long room, a hallway almost that served as kitchen and study. I sat at the tall windows and looked out the back into the neighbor's pool, while I listened to the left behind Bonnie Raitt tapes with the lights off. A glass of wine sweated in my hand and I pretended that I belonged there.

There was this one who lived in the oldest house in the county. She had five cats. We walked over the wide-plank floors from room to room and in her study, she showed me the cedar chest in the corner. Then she turned to me and said that if the house caught on fire, I should first corral the cats and get them into my car. Then I should come back for the cedar chest and take it out of the house. She pantomimed carrying it, though we both knew she meant drag. It was far too heavy to carry.

There was this one with the matching Shih Tzus and the white carpet. Not a good mix. Not a good mix for little dogs that could not control their bladders. Not a good mix for red wine and shaky hands.

And there was this one who, when I met him, had his pants undone and his shirttail sticking out, a five o'clock shadow that was verging on midnight and a stale, vinegary odor all about him. He had an unpleasant aviary off the kitchen, filled with small birds—finches and swallows—and an old shepherd who needed me to give him an enema if he did not shit each day. And there was a macaw in a huge, covered cage in the living room.

I was to take the cover—a pale blue sheet—off the macaw cage every day to give the creature light. I was watching TV when the macaw left its cage, clawed its way out on gnarled feet. It limped and dragged itself toward me. I was--what?--about one million times its size and yet it had me beat. I found a tool, a broom, and went at it, pushing it back toward its cage until it climbed back in, looking at me over its shoulder.

You fucker, it was thinking. You don't belong here. Get out of my house.

The macaw made me feel like our Japanese exchange student. My sister shook his hand first thing and then at dinner she laughed so hard that she squirted milk out her nose. He left the table in tears and was on a plane home the next day.

FREAK
MAGNET

Just look at the pretty young men skulking in the doorways or leaning into car windows with their asses in the air like cats with swishing tails. Just look at them.

"This is it," Rene said. "We're stopping here."

The motor inn was on Peachtree, but then everything was on Peachtree in one way or another because every other street in Atlanta was called Peachtree. And what of these fresh blooming orchards of fresh ripe peaches no longer found on the hot streets of the city? Where had they gone? There were strip mall establishments with ladies modeling lingerie for a fee and drive-thru liquor stores leaking bottles and cigarettes but there were no peach trees.

The inn had fading turquoise walls and a forever bleating "VACANCY" sign and an entrance filled with men in wheelchairs, smoking unfiltered cigarettes and drinking black coffee from flimsy paper cups.

"This is it, my darling," Rene said and held his hand up to Marnie's cheek, petting it gentle as a mother would. Marnie loved the feel of his palm on her face. It was the most human, the most decent of touches. It was a touch she'd know since they had come together in childhood, when Rene was scorned in their neighborhood for his flamboyant ways. Those same ways were what drew Marnie to him like a June bug to a screen—all hard shell and clinging legs, grasping and tugging to be let in. And now here they were in this strange place, alone and together.

*

They had taken to the road in search of Marnie's lost father and the road led them south, away from the pale northern sky and the closed lips of home—no one speaking, no one telling the truth. Cigarette smoke clouded the air inside of the beat-up Mustang the whole way down from Maine through the Mid-Atlantic, hitting the south somewhere below Maryland in an explosion of green, a wall of kudzu. To pass the time Rene sang along with John Denver as massive tractor-trailers carrying plastic lawn chairs, spiral notebooks, and juice boxes shuddered by on their way to the local Wal-Mart.

They stopped at a gun and clothing store next to a Cracker Barrel and each purchased a pair of denim overalls. "You look adorable in those, honey," Rene said as he spun Marnie around in the parking lot in the yellow June light. Her wispy hair floated out around her like a shawl. She spun and saw the mirage of colored leaves above. But there were no other colors than green—green everywhere. So much green that she felt it choking her, a belt around her neck.

In South Carolina, Rene cut the bottoms off his overalls making them shorts. He wore them on top of the paisley leggings Marnie had given him for his last birthday. "You look beautiful," she said and blew him a kiss from the driver's seat. Rene put on a tape of Olivia Newton John and fell asleep with his hand on Marnie's shoulder.

*

In the store, she bought five postcards: Dolly Parton, Minnie Pearl, Johnny Cash, Patsy Cline, and Willie Nelson. These were Rene's people.

He mouthed along with Dolly and Patsy when they sang. He worshipped Minnie's irreverence, her hats. Johnny would be his first husband and Willie his second. They were the ones he adored.

She would use them to speak for her, to offer the words that her mouth could not say. One day she would give them to him and he would know and on that day they would be together forever or they would fall away from each other like bark stripped away from the tree trunk, leaving a bare patch where once there was life.

When they stopped at the Motel 6 for the night and Rene took his shower, she took out Dolly Parton and wrote:

> Dear Rene,
> I believe your skin is made up of stars instead of cells and that you glow like the Milky Way. I see you and I see constellations, galaxies, a black hole. I see everything and nothing.
> Forever yours,
> Marnie

She kissed Dolly Parton's face and tucked the postcard back in her bag with the others.

*

On their first night in Atlanta, they prowled the back streets until they found a multi-level, all-night club. There they met drag queens and the hustlers, frat boys and adventuresome tourists. Marnie felt woozy with the spectacle of it all—men in pantyhose and wigs. Men with breasts and lipsticked lips. Men with their arms wrapped around each other in a perfect embrace. She wanted to sit on her barstool and watch it all night, instead she fell asleep with her head on the bar, oblivious to the non-stop, pounding music.

She woke as a pretty boy in blue spandex bike shorts and push-up bra nudged into her in an attempt to get the attention of the bartender. "'Scuse me, darlin'," he said, not really looking at her. She would have done anything for him to touch her again.

"Sorry." Marnie stood up and squeezed by him. As she did he sized up her breasts with his hands.

He said, "What's it like to be a real woman?"

"I don't know," Marnie said. She still felt like a girl, hapless and without boundaries. She wanted to say something more about how she hoped she'd find out here, in this city, what being a woman meant. How she hoped she would find her father and learn why it was she felt the way she did—empty and without a voice, hollow and blank-faced. But when she opened her mouth to speak to him, he was already gone, his back whisking away into the darkness.

*

On the second level of the club, Marnie chose a chair at an empty table in the corner and pulled the postcard of Minnie Pearl and a pen out of her bag. She chewed on the pen cap while she figured out what to write. She wrote:

> Dear Rene,
> My mother once told me that I was good for nothing but attracting freaks. She said if I kept it up there'd have to be a whole circus devoted to me and my sideshow. In a way, I think she was right. I'm a magnet for the sort who doesn't fit in anywhere. I'm a freak magnet. But the thing is that I think the people who don't fit in are the best ones. Don't you?
> I will always love you,
> Marnie

A man dressed in a purple velvet cape sat next to her, without meeting her gaze, he said, "And you are?" He ran a hand over his glistening curls, slippery, sleek. His accent was not southern, but affected, vaguely British. She couldn't place it.

"Marnie," she said and held out her hand, which he ignored.

"I am Disciple," he said. He was probably a Jesus freak or something and she had done her time with that sort. They were for her mother. Not her. He flicked the sides of his cape back over his shoulders and shifted in his chair so that he faced her. Marnie scanned the tables in search of Rene.

"You seem lost and that moves me." He grabbed one of her hands in his slick palm. Marnie tugged it once but let him keep the hand in his.

"I'm looking for my friend. We came here together."

"But you will leave with me," he said with such assuredness, that she did believe she would leave with him and when her weariness got the better of her, she accepted Disciple's offer of a ride home.

But it wasn't home she was going to—not in the real sense. Home was back up in Maine, on the coast where the wind blew in steady and strong from the cold Atlantic. Home was with her mother and stepfather in too close quarters. Home was where people waited for church, waited for food stamps, waited for retirement, waited to die. She would not be going home.

Instead, she would be going to the Voyager Inn—where she and Rene had found a room for $100 a week—money they'd earned working at Chili's together. The room had a small fridge and a chair and a television, but only one queen bed, which they shared. It was fine for now. It was perfect.

Disciple's car was painfully normal—an old Tempo, pale blue with rusting doors. She'd expected something more elaborate—a decked out hearse, a Rolls-Royce. Something big and colorful. He told Marnie to buckle up and then he took off his cape and folded it gently into the back seat, petting it slightly before he shut the door. Without it, she noticed the paunch below his tightly cinched belt. He was old. Probably her father's age. For all she knew, he could be her father.

"Do you have kids?" she asked.

"No," he said, "are you interested?"

Marnie pushed closer to her door, hand on handle.

"I'm just teasing," he said and patted her knee then turned on the ignition. "You'll be home soon."

She directed him to the inn as best she could but he seemed to know the way. In the parking lot dimly lit by one flickering streetlight, she moved to open her door, but Disciple was turned toward her, his arm was across her, pinning her in the seat. "Payment," he said, softly. He lifted his free hand to her face, caressed her cheek and then moved his fingers back through her hair. When his fingers reached the back of her skull, he pushed against it, pushed forward. She thought he might want a kiss, so she puckered up with tight lips. She could get through that. It wouldn't be the worst thing that had happened to her and then she and Rene could laugh about it afterwards. She could just hear him, shrieking, "You kissed that old queen?"

"No, no," Disciple said, grasping her head, moving his other hand down to his lap. She heard his zipper and looked down despite herself. There, below her and coming closer as he pushed her head down, was his penis encased in a diamond-studded thong. "Be nice," he said.

There was nothing to do. No choice. She tried to think how she could make this funny for Rene. She tried to think how they would laugh about it. Nothing came to mind as she took the soft thing in her mouth, sour and cold at the tip. "No biting," Disciple said. "That's right. That's nice."

Nothing came to mind.

Later, she sat on the bathroom floor by the toilet, waiting to throw up again. When nothing else would come, she took out Johnny Cash and her pen and wrote:

Dear Rene,

I wish one day that we would have our own house together. A ranch out West where we raised horses, Appaloosas. And we would ride them all day and come home with the sun setting behind us in a wash of orange and pink. At night, we'd sing songs by the campfire and no one would ever be afraid to be alone.
I'm gonna love you 'til the end of time,
Marnie

She crawled into bed next to Rene, his back to her. On his other side was the person he'd brought home, a boy not much older than they were, sleeping with his arm over his eyes. Rene murmured, "Did you have fun, Princess?"

"Yes," Marnie said and turned on her side to bury her face into the cool spot between Rene's shoulder blades.

"Who's that?" the boy, awakened, asked.

"It's just Princess," Rene said.

The boy pushed up on his elbows and looked at her. "Wow," he said. "I haven't been in bed with a girl in, like, forever."

"Well, don't get yourself all worked up, fella," Rene said yawning. "She's not here for fun, just to sleep. If you're nice she might even say hi to you, but she doesn't talk much." He reached a hand back and patted her hip, said, "Always been a quiet one, my Princess." Marnie touched her lips to the skin on Rene's back and exhaled. It was something like a kiss.

*

The search for Marnie's father began on the second day in Atlanta and entailed deciphering the words written in her mother's hand on a yellowing piece of paper. Marnie found the note three years prior, as she pawed through her mother's things, organizing them for a tag sale they were throwing to earn rent money. At the bottom of an old leather purse that she had never seen her mother use, she found the scrap of paper. It said:

Five points. Harry. Organ.

She focused on the paper until everything else was black and it was just her breathing and the words. With shaking hands she folded and carefully placed it in her bra lest anyone discover it.

She hadn't mentioned it to anyone until the day of graduation from high school, when she and Rene celebrated by eating chocolate cupcakes underneath the big tree in the yard—the tree where Marnie had kissed Rene for the first time and he had laughed at her, thinking it was a joke.

She did not think of that soft kiss as she showed Rene the note and he asked her, "What do you suppose it means?"

"Harry," Marnie said between licks of frosting, "is my real dad. The one who ran away."

"Okay."

"And five points. I think that means Little Five Points." Rene motioned for her to continue. "It's a neighborhood in Atlanta. In Georgia."

"I want to be a southern belle. You know that. Don't tease." Rene stood up and sashayed, waving an imaginary fan.

"This isn't about you," Marnie said, folding the note back into its creases. She felt bad as soon as she said it, because it was about him in a way.

"Oh, honey. I'm just having fun." Rene dropped to his knees in front of her. "Go on and tell me about the rest." But she couldn't because she didn't know the rest. Organ could mean anything and Marnie could not let go of her belief that it had some deeper meaning, was some explanation of what had happened to her father. On a late June day when the grass was turning from spring green to the darkness of summer, they loaded up the Mustang and followed the path Marnie had highlighted with yellow ink in the Atlas. The path led them down the highway from state to state until it snaked through the details of the city and ended at Little Five Points.

*

They stumbled along the streets of Little Five Points filled with kids doused in patchouli, jugglers in striped pants, Rastafarians in knit caps and old poets with baggy knees, until Marnie, overwhelmed, sat down on the curb. She felt lost and a wave of homesickness for her mother's soft hands washing her back when she was just small overcame her.

"What is it?" Rene said. "Did you see him?" She shook her head.

"What are we doing here?" She wondered why she had been so set on this search. Wasn't sure what she'd even say to a father if she had one.

"Honey, I don't know and I've got a splitting headache. I'm going to get an iced coffee." He left Marnie sitting on the curb. She pulled out Patsy Cline and a pen. She wrote:

> Dear Rene,
> I wonder what would have happened if my father had never run away. Do you think you and I would never have become friends? Do you think that if we had, we still would have gone on a trip together? Maybe we would have gone to Europe instead. Or maybe we would have rode out of town like Bonnie and Clyde with our guns blazing.
> I love you so much (it hurts),
> Marnie

A man dressed in khakis and loafers, a normal man who could have been someone's dad or high school principal, stopped short when he saw her, squatted down and bounced on his heels. "You look hot," he said. Marnie squinted up at him and smiled. "So do you like to party or what?"

Marnie felt the light and air suck in and out around her, fluttering baby lungs. She looked down.

"I said, do you like to party? Like, how much?" He rubbed his thumb and forefinger together in front of her nose. She felt dizzy in the sun until she saw Rene tripping back across the street.

"There's my friend," she nodded towards Rene who was teetering through a throng of tourists on his platform shoes. "My boyfriend."

"Oh, yeah? Okay then." He was gone, disappeared as if he had never been there.

"Little girl, are you lost?" Rene asked as he handed her a sweating iced coffee and sat down beside her. "Didn't your mother ever teach you not to take candy from strangers?" Rene chuckled and pumped his straw in and out of the lid of his coffee several times, producing an ear splitting eeek-eeek sound.

"So I asked in the coffee shop about Harry's organ," Rene said. "And the lovely young man with the precious dimples suggested that it might mean or-GAN-ic. There's a grocer the next street over." Rene stood up and offered Marnie his hand. "Shall we?"

*

Vines clung to the brick building and the sign, lettered in purple paint, read, "Harry's Organics and Sundries."

"Well, I guess this is it," Rene said, squeezing her hand and smiling. "Let's go," Rene said. "Come on."

"I can't." She wanted to throw her coffee at the window and bolt down the street. Instead, she turned around and walked back the way they had come.

"I'm going anyway," Rene yelled behind her. "I'm going to meet your maker, Marnie."

She looked at him where he stood, arms crossed, one foot bent at a crooked angle, uncomfortable, hot, and possibly afraid.

Marnie walked back and used her sleeve to wipe her sticky forehead. "Come on, Marnie," he said. "What's it going to hurt?"

She wanted to say that it would hurt everything. That if she went through that door she might cease to exist entirely, all words gone. Still, she felt a slight tug within her that maybe the answer did lie within that store. Perhaps all that was her reality—her past and her present—was there among the wheat grass juice and Power Bars.

She let him lead her through the door. There was a girl with purple dreadlocks, picking her nails behind the cash register. She glanced at them as they walked in but said nothing. The floor was dusty and the air smelled peppery, like sweat and bread baking, not entirely unpleasant. Rene walked over to the register and asked the girl, "Is Harry here?"

"What?" The girl lifted her head. Rene motioned Marnie over to him but she felt she couldn't move. Instead, she stood on the other side, watching the girl's hair from behind. She had heard of some guy who had bugs living in his dreadlocks. He'd been that way for months and not realized it until the itching became too much. She wondered if the girl took care of herself, cleansed her scalp. Marnie pictured her hands massaging through the dreadlocks, spreading oil on the thin skin of the scalp.

Rene put his hands on his hips, frowned at Marnie. "Is Harry here?" he asked again.

"There is no Harry, dude," the girl said, slowly, evenly. Her voice was pretty, it was a poetry voice. Marnie thought of this dreadlock girl at an open mic, reciting something painful and private. Something about love or loss. Something about believing in one thing and finding another.

"No Harry?" Rene said. "Are you sure?" Marnie could see the blood in his cheeks—this happened just before the tears. She went to him, put an arm around his waist. Met the dreadlock girl face to face.

"Yeah, I'm sure. No Harry. He was the original guy, owner, whatever, back when they started in 1972 or whatever, but he, like, died. Immediately. Didn't even get to see the paint dry on the sign. Or whatever." The girl's voice got softer as she spoke until it was almost a whisper and they had to lean in to catch the end of her words.

"Oh," Rene said, throwing off Marnie's arm. "Well, that's just super. Thanks for nothing." Rene stormed down the aisle and out the door, trying for a slam but it eased shut with a tinkle of the bell behind him. Marnie watched as he walked out of view. She should have gone right after him. Should have followed him right out of the store. There was no reason to stay.

"Sorry," she said to the girl. "He gets like that."

"That's cool," the girl said, smiling.

"We were looking for someone. For my father. We thought Harry might be him. But he couldn't be. Can't be. Because my father would have been in Maine then, getting my mother pregnant. He was a welder, I think. Something like that. Anyway, he wouldn't have been here. Wouldn't have been running a store then. It just doesn't fit. Anyway, we drove all the way here from Maine to find him. But it's not him." It was too bad. She had grown fond of the idea of her father, pressing out carrots for juice, taking dietary supplements. She had thought he might have taught her how to live well, eat properly, drink water, get sleep, exercise.

"Sucks," the girl said, "Sorry."

"It's okay," Marnie said.

"We're playing tonight," the girl handed her a blue flyer, an advertisement for a band. As Marnie took the flyer, the girl's fingers lingered on her wrist. "You should come."

"Maybe I will," Marnie said. She left then but not before she turned back and smiled at the dreadlock girl, hair backlit from the cooler, glowing ropes.

Later on a bench in the sun, she took out Willie Nelson and wrote:

Dear Rene,

*Whenever I am not with you, I pretend I have your hand in mine
and you are right there walking beside me or lying in bed, always
talking, always reminding me that I am never alone.*

*If I was a mother, you would be my child. If I was a daughter,
you would be my father. If I drove a tractor trailer, you would be
my favorite mixed tape. If I was a lover, you would be my love.*

But I am none of these.

Just remember this.

I will love you always,

Marnie

She took out all of the postcards and read them one by one. They were
stamped and addressed to Rene care of the Voyager Inn. She found a
mailbox nearby, opened the lid and held them over the edge, then let them
fall one by one into the darkness below.

THE
VILLAGER

We lived at The Villager for a month or more. Two double beds covered in slippery, pilled spreads, and a dingy mini-fridge. We were allowed to smoke in the room. When Sylvie came to visit, she shared Martin's bed and I kept my own. Sylvie had a floppy-eared stuffed bunny with her. She clutched it at night and spoke with a lisp.

She often asked if I would like to feel her breasts.

No, I said, I would not.

*

From the site to The Villager was an uphill walk. Once we saw a woman's umbrella turn inside out in the wind. Without knowledge, she moved into the street trying to right the fabric.

I asked Martin what it was called, the fabric.

Fabric, he said.

We watched as a car struck her, gently, knocked her down, and moved on. She was prone, and then sitting, legs splayed, swaying. She stood up and left her umbrella behind.

When we passed, Martin kicked it into the gutter. Bad luck. Back lud.

*

The French Canadians lived in temporary housing. Even though their Thanksgiving was long past, the French Canadians cooked us a chicken and held a celebration in our honor.

Salut! Ca va?

Ca va.

*

I left The Villager and went downtown to meet Frederic at his hotel. We sat on stools in a well-lit bar and drank rum and Coke.

Later, I joined him in his room. From up that high, you could see all the lights of the city, but you could not see the lights of The Villager.

He fucked me without a condom. I wondered if I would die.

*

There was a man, alone, next door to our room. His glasses tinted black when he was out in the light.

What I told Martin was this: That I saw the man dragging a large suitcase to the parking garage.

What we speculated was this: Within that suitcase was a body.

Body of a girl. A female body about my size, my age.

A body bag.

*

The Villager never felt like home. Not even when we took turns kissing Sylvie. Not even when Martin pretended he was a member of the Hair Club for Men.

It never felt like home and I waited to be carried out, to be lugged out in a bag by a man with black-covered eyes. I waited to be discarded by him.

Not even when the sky got gray and grayer and rain fell did it feel like home. It felt like a place we should be leaving. It felt like a place we had already left.

THE EMERGENCY CONTACT

The accident that killed Craig was stupid. It happened in the windowless break room where he was reading *Rolling Stone*. On the cover was David Lee Roth wearing yellow shorts, a Hawaiian shirt, suspenders and, of course, a big white hat. The guy was freakishly flamboyant—so unlike Craig's favorite, the sedate and yet smiling Eddie Van Halen.

As Craig regarded the glazed eyes and open mouth on the cover he relaxed into his favorite fantasy—that Lee Roth left the band (as was rumored he would do) and that the other members came looking for him—for Craig—to fill the spot as lead singer. It's not that he was such a great singer but he did believe he had the charisma to pull it off and he thought Eddie would think so too. Then they buzzed him from up front. Prish, the new guy, had to void a sale on a pinstripe suit and suspenders. Couldn't people remember for three seconds how to do anything? Did they always have to interrupt his break? There were so few joys working retail, and break was one of them—a private moment for reflecting on outside interests, having a leisurely smoke, drinking a Tab or taking a shit.

More often than not, Craig's break was ruined by just this sort of thing—someone else's incompetence. He threw the magazine across the room, where it hit the cement wall and slid to the floor. Then he stood up, straightened his tie, tugged at his vest, lifted his jacket from the back of an orange plastic chair where he'd placed it earlier and put it on, one arm at a time. Then Craig walked with determination toward the door.

The problem was the magazine.

It was on the floor and even though he threw it there a few seconds prior, he had forgotten about it.

The magazine was open, with its spine exposed, and as Craig's gray tap shoes hit the cover, he slid. And as he slid he waved his arms in wide circles (this is what they saw on the video recording later—Anderson-Little being a test market for the video recorded security devices which were soon to be used at the new South Hills Mall) in an almost comical way. In fact, some of the folks—security officials, police officers and Anderson-Little management—watching the tape had chuckled until they realized that the kid had died.

Still it was funny.

So the arms were spinning for-what-seemed-like-ever and then he went down—quick, clean. A quick, clean smack of head against concrete break room floor. And it was over.

*

There was a message written in purple ink on a piece of paper towel taped to the bathroom mirror. It said: "Megan, Someone called for you and said that something has happened to Craig! Something Bad!!" And there was a final line that suggested action: "Call the store!!!"

Megan wasn't sure which one of her roommates wrote the message— Peggy? Lori? —as the writer had not identified herself and Megan hadn't known the two of them long enough to recognize the handwriting. But that was neither here nor there. Something bad had happened.

Of course, she wanted to yell, "Is he dead?" but she didn't. No one would have heard her. She had just gotten home from work and she was alone,

Peggy and Lori having left hours before for their cocktail waitress jobs at Casey's, the dingy little bar next to the North Hills Mall. She pulled the note down from the toothpaste-speckled mirror, held it with both hands and shook it, gritting her teeth, wanting it to give her more details.

She moved from the bathroom down the dimly lit hallway to her bedroom where she recovered her blue princess phone from beneath a pile of discarded clothing and punched in the numbers to Craig's store. She felt inappropriately excited by the situation—anxious, elated almost—and wasn't sure whether she should sit or stand, so instead of doing either, she knelt next to her bed and rested her forehead against the rough fabric of her comforter—a cheap, floral thing her mother had bought her at Woolworth when they all still thought Megan was going to college.

Four rings and someone picked up, a man. "Hello?"

"I got a message? About Craig?" Skin dry and cracked from the early spring cold, little snags caught on her fingers as she ran her hand over the pilled comforter.

"Who is this?" The man's voice accusatory, as though she'd done something wrong.

"Megan? Craig's girlfriend?" Her voice pitched out of her—uncertain, babyish. She hated herself when she sounded this way.

"Oh." The man covered the phone. There was a muffled conversation and then another man came on. "Megan?"

"Yes," she said. "Yes, that's me." She lifted her head, joy spreading through her, as if she'd won something.

"Craig had you listed as the emergency contact."

"Oh," she said.

"And we need you to help us get in touch with the family." The man's voice was tired now, deflated. Sort of the way Craig used to sound after a day at Anderson-Little, pissed at himself for not quitting. Pissed at himself for not living the life of the starving artist and giving it all up for his music.

Pissed and wiped out and dead inside. But why used to? Why did she all of a sudden think in the past about Craig?

"What's wrong? Where's Craig? " Her voice rising, rising and ears growing hot.

"I'm going to need you to calm down, Megan. Can you do that for me?" Now he sounded like her General Manager, Cal—always so in charge and parental. Always telling people how to feel.

"What's going on?" she said. She wanted to say, "I demand to know what is going on" but stopped herself because she thought that sounded too wifely or too like something you would hear on Quincy, maybe with Angie Dickinson as sexy special guest star—the sexy wife whose husband died. And maybe she would go to Quincy, the forensic pathologist, and demand to know what is going on, only to later end up on his boat with him, confessing how she never really loved her husband, giving Quincy that little hair of a clue to know what she was up to and to regret that he had ever let down his guard and allowed her into his life. He would know she had done it. But it was too late. Quincy was canceled a few years before and she wasn't even sure if Angie Dickinson had ever been a guest star.

"Megan, honey, there is no easy way to say this. I'm afraid there has been an accident." Accident? "Craig didn't make it." He didn't make it.

"Oh," Megan said and then there was only the sound coming out of her mouth—a squeal, high and light and fine. It pulled up from her gut and spun out of her mouth like a worm. It wound its way through the phone line to the man's ear on the other end, forcing itself into his mouth and pushing his words back at him so that they would never be spoken again.

*

Craig had been the manager at Anderson-Little for two years. Anderson-Little, which sold men's tailored clothing, was located at the North Hill's Mall, nestled between Montgomery Ward and Kay-Bee Toy and Hobby, which is where, up until three weeks prior, Megan had worked. She was a manager as well—although not for as long as Craig had been. Only just a few months. And it was thanks to her managerial position at North Hills that she now had a job in the new mall, South Hills, across the highway from North. "We know you can do it, Kid," is what Cal said to her. "I bet you feel on top of the world." And she had felt special, sort of. South Hills had skylights, a megaplex, a food court and theme restaurants.

But Craig had stayed behind at North. And now that's what he would always be, Craig from North Hills. The one who died on break.

*

When Megan started working at North, she had noticed Craig. How could she not? He was gorgeous and sleek like a fisher she'd seen poking its face out from the woods once when she was still a child and on a walk with her mother. She'd wanted to touch that fisher's long, sinewy body. To let it wrap around her neck and poke its mousey face into her own, a small tongue darting out and lingering on her cheek. She had tried to follow the creature into the woods, but her mother had advised against it, "They look pretty but they're mean," she had said. "Bite you, as soon as look at you." Still, the desire to hunt down and stroke the slippery fisher had been strong and Megan had harkened back to that feeling many times over the years until it came to stand for desire. It was the same feeling she had when she first saw Craig. She wanted to find out his secret places, to cajole him into kindness, to wear him like a fur stole.

For months, Megan watched Craig striding by with his Key Bank bag tucked under his arm, going for change. Observed him at S'barro eating a slice for lunch every day and lingered near his table at Casey's Pub, where he drank pitchers and discussed this stupid customer or that stupid customer with his staff. But she hadn't had the guts to talk to him.

Craig was older, around 23, and was the type of guy who would drive a Trans Am or maybe even a Monte Carlo with tinted windows. He wore any number of Anderson-Little three-piece suits to work every day. Whereas Megan felt shabby in her Kay-Bee uniform—white shirt and blue slacks—dressed up for holidays with a blinking pumpkin pin or red Santa cap. She hated being in the same room with Craig in his suits and the girls from the clothing stores like Purple Banana and Women's Intuition in their Z. Carravici's and angora sweaters. But when she first made manager and started going to the North Hills managers' functions—monthly meetings, happy hours, etc—she noticed that maybe Craig was noticing her. More than once, she'd caught him staring at her across the table at the monthly meeting. She knew she wasn't ugly, far from it; in fact, people often said she looked like the girl who was the alcoholic in that after school special. No one knew the actress' name but when people saw Megan, they would more often than not comment on the striking resemblance, saying, "Hey! You know who you look like? That girl. The drunk one."

Oddly, she wasn't as surprised as she thought she would be when Craig did ask her out for a drink after one of the meetings. They shared a couple of pitchers at Casey's and ended up back at his place—an unexpectedly shabby studio with an unmade bed and an electric guitar in the corner and a half dozen posters of Eddie Van Halen on the walls.

"Do you play?" Megan asked stupidly and hoped he wouldn't make fun of her.

But he smiled and pulled her to him. "Let's not talk," he said. "Not until later." Then they had sex, quickly, inexpertly. She had pictured doing it with Craig for so long that it turned out to be something of a disappointment. He was too eager to get on with it, jabbing into her and then slipping out, wet and sleepy.

"What are you thinking about?" Craig said afterwards, pulling her into a snuggle.

"Nothing."

"I want to be Eddie Van Halen," Craig said, gazing at a poster of Eddie and his guitar, which had watched over them as they fucked. "I love him."

"Yeah. He's really great." Megan was hurt that his interest in her thoughts was fleeting.

"If he asked me, I'd have sex with him."

"Oh." She wondered if Eddie would enjoy it with Craig more than she had.

"He's a genius." Craig jumped out of bed then, picked up his guitar and played Running with the Devil three times from start to finish. Megan lay back and listened. She wasn't sure what else to do.

*

Craig didn't have any family. He had been a foster kid and his last set of foster parents was dead—this was what the agency had said when Megan called them. It had been up to her, then, as emergency contact and girlfriend of two months to put together the funeral. Anderson-Little was paying for everything—they insisted on it—, which was helpful since Craig's workmen's comp check was held in some sort of limbo—the netherworld of the family-less employee. But truly, workmen's comp being what it is, Anderson-Little was much better off that Craig had died instead of suffering some sort of brain damage that would keep him in some sort of expensive vegetative state for years.

The GM Megan spoke to said, "Craig was one of our finest. He was going places." She had wanted to say something inappropriate, like how much Craig hated Anderson-Little. How he was milking his gig there until his band, Jamie's Cryin', took off, but she didn't. She listened to the guy and then told him how much money she would need. "Just send me the bills," he said. "Anything for Craig. But let's not go crazy and get the most expensive casket—so within reason is what I'm saying. Within reason."

Megan didn't know anything about picking out a casket. She brought one of her roommates with her but wasn't sure which one as she had passed the point where she could politely ask them their names. Together, she and Lori/Peggy had chosen a white casket with purple interior and when going over details Megan asked the funeral director if it was okay if Craig was buried with his guitar. She thought Craig would like that and felt satisfied with her choice to include it. Felt also sort of a lifting of the odd feeling that had been tapping on her shoulder. The one that came to her at night when she was alone and whispered to her that it was all her fault.

*

People told her she was holding up beautifully. When he swung by to check on her at South Hills, Cal said he would have thought she would be bawling, losing her first love like that. "You'll never have another like him," Cal said and hugged awkwardly. Then he held her at arm's length and said, "You are holding up beautifully, Kid. The whole Kay Bee organization is proud of you." She didn't feel they should be proud of her, necessarily. She was doing what she had to do as the emergency contact.

Other than her reaction when she found out that Craig was dead, she was pretty much like this—moving forward and getting things done. Her emotion or lack thereof was less a sense of wanting to hold up beautifully and more because she had known Craig would die. Had expected it or, more appropriately, had wanted it because she had started to think, at some point, that it would be easier than breaking up with him.

Early on, it became apparent to Megan that there was a tipping of the scales in their relationship, that it might be possible that he actually liked her more than she liked him, a notion she would never have believed to be true, but which eventually seemed undeniable.

Megan grew to feel that Craig was a sort of a hologram of himself or the self she had thought he was. Initially, she thought she would always feel that thrill she felt when she first saw him, those crazy fingers in her belly poking her from the inside out, pushing her to him. But then she was ashamed for him. Ashamed that he had stayed behind at North Hills and she wondered if he had moved over to South Hills like she had if she wouldn't have started to see Craig's suits for what they were—crappy suits from a crappy North Hills store.

But South Hills didn't have an Anderson-Little—it was like a dying store, past its time. There was no room for it in the sparkling new mall, rather it was relegated to low-ceilinged lesser-mall, with anchor stores like K-Mart and JC Penney. So Craig couldn't have moved even if he wanted to. He was trapped at North Hills and he didn't even seem to care. It was all about the band and the two of them living the high life when he made it to the top.

Once when they lay side by side on his musty bed, Craig had said to her, "We'll have a laser light show like no one has ever seen. And one of the lights will spell out Megan on the roof of the arena. Your name will hang there in the air and then disappear slowly but it will be burned into everyone's eyes." But she hadn't wanted her name burned into anyone's eyes. She felt panicked at the thought, actually. That people would know her as his girlfriend and that was the only way they would know her. Forever. She would be Craig's girl, his Megan.

The lasers would be like prison bars, fleeting but trapping her nonetheless.

But Megan had never broken up with anyone. Never dreamed she would want to break up with someone. Certainly not Craig. All that time she spent wishing that he would notice her and then when he did, it was not what she expected. She felt like she was noticing herself. Like she was dating and having sex with herself—not someone other, not someone special.

She wondered if it would have been the same for Craig if he had been with Eddie Van Halen. He might have that same sense that this person you imagined sitting beside you in the car when you were listening to your favorite song and who got it, like you got it and who was as into you as you were him but then when it happens all you feel is dead inside. Dead and lonely and you wish that you hadn't been so quick to discard your mother's advice about going to college and staying on the right track. You wish you hadn't dropped out and slept for 20 hours a day in your childhood bedroom because it felt comfortable and safe. You wish that you hadn't yelled at your mother and your grandmother about what the fuck did they know and then gotten yourself kicked out of the house and had to move in with strangers you couldn't tell apart. And you wish that you weren't in the situation where the guy you used to have a crush on worked in some dingy store in the old mall. She wondered if it would have been like that for Craig and Eddie.

But maybe not.

They told Megan that Craig was smiling when he died so there probably wasn't much pain. But she liked to think maybe the smile was about meeting Eddie and having it be just exactly what Craig expected—two musical geniuses coming together, exploding in the sky, melting like stars.

She hoped, more than anything, he wasn't thinking about her.

HE
DIED

On the day Charles Bukowski died, Marla was working the register. Jackson, furious in his grief, rapidly piled the front table with all the Bukowski the store had in stock. Then he made a sign in big black letters that said, "Charles Bukowski: He died. So we're having a sale."

He faced the sign out to the street.

Some people got it and others were offended by the sign.

It was funny. It was Bukowski.

"How could you?" One woman came off the street to say. "The man died." She was quite angry.

Jackson gave her the blank stare, kept his hands in his pockets.

"Well?" the woman pushed.

"He's dead all right," Jackson said. "Dead." The woman waited for a few seconds longer and turned to leave, saying she would not shop there again as she pushed out the door.

As if she ever had.

Marla felt a bit sorry for the woman and also sorry for Charles Bukowski because he had died. And after what kind of life? His enormous, purple-veined nose was gone, decomposing.

She had read enough Bukowski, sure, but not nearly as much as Jackson had. Like most young men she knew, Jackson felt a kinship to Bukowski. There was a brotherhood. Jackson felt like he could act the way he really wanted to act because of Bukowski. He didn't have to love her.

"You can go on break now," Jackson said when three girls on their way home from high school entered the store.

She heard them asking him about Bukowski. Who was he and which of his books were good. They'd been in the store before. She knew the tall, black-haired one was the reason. She wanted Jackson.

Marla was small and pale and unremarkable. Her bones felt like Q-tips beneath her skin. That was something Jackson had said to her once. A moment of poetry. Or so he thought.

Her nails were bitten, but Jackson didn't notice that. He noticed the blue veins on her temples. The veins of a toddler, he said. A young, young child.

They had been lying on her futon mattress when Jackson said this to her about her veins. Marla had squashed the mattress beneath the one window in her studio, so that she could read with the light of the streetlamp and not waste money on electricity. She was proud that her electric bill was so low, her needs so few.

Jackson always came to her place instead of going back to his because he had roommates and she lived closer to the store. He often came over after he'd gone out without her even. "Mind if I crash?" he'd ask as he took off his boots, already assuming the answer.

She sat on one of the plastic chairs in the book closet which doubled as their break room. In her cubby, was the paper sack lunch she'd prepared for herself earlier in the day. She pulled out a can of peaches and unstuck the lid. She used a plastic spoon to feed herself the peaches. They were soft and sugary in her mouth. A new tongue lying upon her old tongue.

She heard the hyper vibration of Jackson's voice. He was excited, wowing them with his knowledge of Bukowski, making them laugh.

She bit through the slice of peach in her mouth, chewed and swallowed it. Took in another and let it lie there. The tongue would speak for her. She would keep it there until she saw Jackson again.

BUDDHIST

Bucky came home with his hair shaved off almost the whole way, right down to the scalp. White skin shiny and stretched over his bumpy head. When I asked him why he cut it, he said it was because he wanted to be a Buddhist.

If a mosquito bit him, he would not kill it, he said.

His hair was no longer of relevance to him, he said.

It was merely vanity that kept it on his head so long, he said.

He was glad it was gone, he said.

It made his face look different—pointed, beaky, dry. Not at all like he was when I first saw him hanging out in the alcove outside the Harvard T-stop. That day his hair had been chin length and when he looked at me, his cheeks were just the palest dusk of a dogwood bloom.

He leaned his skateboard up against the wall but it slid down and rolled across the wood floor, almost to exactly the spot in front of where I was sitting in the nubby chair we'd dragged home from last week's trash picking. I reached my foot out and snagged the board, placed both feet on it and rolled it back and forth.

A Buddhist, I said.

Yes, Bucky said and went into the bathroom and turned on the shower.

He left me sitting there with his skateboard, wondering if he'd let me use his laptop now that he was a Buddhist. Wondering if he would still get pissed off if I put his albums back out of alphabetical order. Wondering if he would kill me if I bit him.

Do Buddhists have sex? I yelled.

What?

Do they have sex? I rolled the skateboard this or that way with each word. Four times. Waiting for his answer.

The shower ran on, squealing through the old pipes.

Do they? I rolled the skateboard twice. Have sex? Twice more.

I don't know, Bucky said. I guess.

Okay, I said, and gave the skateboard one last roll away from me.

Okay what?

You are a Buddhist.

I wasn't asking permission, he said, standing in the doorway, a towel around his waist, his slick head glistening.

Come here and let me feel that head, I said. And he did. He came right over to me and knelt at my feet, bending his head forward, a proper monk. I ran my hands back and forth over the velvet head and then I kissed it.

God bless you, my son, I said. He raised his head and he kissed me on the lips. It was the first time I had ever been kissed by a Buddhist. I felt the orange light within him snake through his mouth into mine. We were high above the world then. On a mountain in Tibet. His hands were not hands but wings beating against me. The air was so sparse that our breath whispered back into our mouths to feed us. We were two mosquitoes meeting, proboscis to proboscis.

And I thought, Amen. Amen.

VERBATIM

The night before I arrived, a hurricane battered the city—knocking down trees, tearing off roofs, displacing puppies. I wouldn't have known about the storm but for the oak tree thrown down—ass up—in the side yard.

Mrs. B, an orange cat in her arms, came out to greet me as I unloaded my things. I'd left home before sunrise, easing through the worn streets, noting every burning light above every kitchen sink, every shadow in every doorway, every tree branch sagging low.

"Big storm," Mrs. B said. "You're lucky you missed it, Jeannie."

Back home I left a garden with tomatoes rotting on the vine, a box of my father's clothes in the basement, and my mother in her housecoat waving to me from the gravel driveway.

But here, in this new town, I missed the storm.

*

The inhabitants of the boarding house shared a kitchen, bathrooms, and common areas, but my room was mine alone. I put a quilt made up of hexagonal pieces on my bed. It had been sewn by my mother's mother back when she was a girl before the Great Depression. The heavy quilt felt like half a dozen tigers were lying on top of me at night, panting, waiting for me to move so they could dig in. I enjoyed pulling the quilt up over my head when I was in bed. I would pretend that I was hiding in a tent, waiting for someone to find me and rescue me before I was smothered by the weight of a stranger with a pillow in his fists, or before I was mauled by big cats.

It was a Victorian rehab, the house, owned by Mrs. B's only son—a would-be real estate developer. Bums and drunks and druggies had lived there once—smeared their shit on the walls, pissed in the corners. But now it was redone, back, almost, to its original glory. Of course, it was in the worst part of town—smack in the middle of South Main. No one would buy it once it was refurbished; hence, the boarding house. I shared the downstairs bathroom with the handyman, one of the old inhabitants now rehabilitated along with the building we lived in.

At night, I sat on the porch with the handyman and watched the hookers walk by. Until one of them was found floating in the murky pond across the street from campus on the Wednesday of my first week in town. And then everything changed.

*

Jared was my sixth appointment on my first day at the university's Voice and Sound Center. He could quote, verbatim, the entire screenplay from "Vision Quest" and he preferred to fuck me with the lights off. "You look better that way," he said.

What drew me to him was his alleged speech impediment—a stutter that no one ever heard. In fact, his stutter was so imperceptible that it was barely a stutter at all. I didn't hear it when he quoted freely from "Vision Quest," thus I was able to meet his eye, clap him on the back.

But why "Vision Quest"? It was certainly an obscure choice of film to memorize. Why not "Casablanca"? Even "Caddyshack" would have been understandable.

I had only seen "Vision Quest" the once and then only for the Madonna cameo when she sang "Crazy for You" in the club scene. Regardless, the plot stuck with me. The main character is a young man—a high school wrestler with a dream of not only beating the odds, but of winning the girl—an enigmatic older woman, new to town, with a sketchy past in tow.

It was, then, much like a young stutterer winning over his speech therapist and fucking her beneath the psychedelic posters in his filthy off-campus apartment.

*

Grasshoppers clung to the screens those early days of September. Up close, I could see the hairiness of their legs, their searchless eyes. Mrs. B said they were trying to tell us something. Perhaps another storm was coming. Perhaps something about the dead woman floating in the pond.

The dead woman. I pulled the quilt up at night and saw her as she would have been in the end: pale limbs outstretched, bloated face nearly unrecognizable, shoes gone, fingernails in tatters.

I felt I should know her name if nothing else, but until I knew her name, I would know her as Carla—same as the love interest in "Vision Quest." The dead woman's hair was Carla-like. Black like the crow—scrappy, fierce. The downtrodden crow with its naked, naked heart.

A hawk lived in the tall white pine trees back home. He tormented the crows, seeking their young. Each summer afternoon, I watched him circling in the blue. Then he was gone, diving. Before long the crows would pick up their wheedling, frantic cries, which tugged at the hearts of the local mothers who otherwise loathed the crows for their early morning chorus.

"I wish that hawk would leave their babies alone!" the mothers (including my own) said.

Soon two or sometimes three crows would chase the hawk away from their nests. Whether he had a baby crow in his talons was open to debate. If the crows took up cawing and carrying on when they made it back to their nests, we figured they were down a head or two. We cursed the hawk, then, circling, squealing victorious in the sky.

*

On the Thursday of my first week, my mother called to ask why hadn't I telephoned to let her know I'd made it all right? "I left a message," I said. But she hadn't spoken to me directly. She was certain there was a problem.

I told her there's no problem and she said, "I should have had another baby after you, Jeannie. That other baby would never up and leave me."

"What would you have named her?"

"How would I know?"

"What about Carla?"

*

Jared brought me a candy apple he bought at the street fair put on by a sorority in order to raise money for childhood obesity awareness. "Apple for the teacher," he said, with no audible stutter. The thing he handed me was a slick red, an impossible red, a poisonous red.

"Where did it come from?"

"I bought it from one of the booths," he said.

This was not like the church bazaar back home, where you knew whose bake goods to avoid. Here I pictured a squalid kitchen—rodents, bugs, droppings. Hair, mucus. There might even be a razor blade embedded inside. It might even be laced with drugs—perhaps something to bring on visions.

I ate the apple and Jared watched as I did. Watched as my teeth cracked through the candy shell and as I licked the bloody stickiness off my lips and fingers.

"See, Jeannie?" he said. "It was good, right?"

"Delicious," I said.

*

It was dark that Tuesday night when Carla died, was murdered. The moon had blown out to sea with the storm, never to return or so it felt on that black, black night. No more harvest moon, no more wolf moon. No more moon, no more.

Carla waited in the doorway of the copy shop, somewhere to lean and she liked the cool glass of the door against her back while she waited for a car to drive by, slow down.

She was tired; she was over it. She had a sick mother with a colostomy bag. Her dog needed a rabies shot. She had forgotten to buy toilet paper. Everything. Her roof leaked. A broken lock. A flat tire. All of it was piling up.

But she didn't know she was going to die, otherwise she might have enjoyed her last moments of life—might have listened more carefully to the breeze which frisked the leaves of the trees lining the street, planted in the name of beautification.

The pimp watched her from a distance, watched as car after car passed by without Carla so much as making an attempt to secure any business. He wad pissed at her lack of ambition. He expected more from Carla. She was one of his top earners. He didn't know her thoughts were elsewhere. He got out of his car and was about to make his way over to her when she made her move. When she got into the other car. The one.

And that's where it ends for me. My vision depleted, sooted over with grief.

*

Jared cancelled his appointments and stopped coming to the center for help. When I questioned him about it over the phone, he told me that he was healed.

"You saved me," he said.

"I never even heard you stutter," I said. "Not once."

"See?" he said. "Cured."

A week before my father died, our yard was overrun by grackles. They pecked at late summer's fallen acorns and downed twigs. They scratched at the dry soil looking for sustenance; the long summer days had been arid, dusty. It was a drought, the newscasters said. I stood at the window over the kitchen sink and counted the grackles. I got to fifty before I lost count and had to start over again.

Soon mother was out in the yard, swinging her broom, yelling at the grackles, "Be gone!"

They flew, en masse, into the popples and white cedars that lined our back fence and waited there for her to leave. But she would not go.

*

I took to spending all of my free nights on the porch, watching. Of special interest was the sugar maple in the lot of the derelict house across the street. My father had taught me how to tap the maples back home for their sap, which we would bring to the sugar shack to turn into syrup. We would put the hot syrup on the snow and wait for it to harden so we could eat it, sugar on snow.

This city maple had bottom branches that were full of glossy leaves yet, just barely turning with the coming autumn, but up top its gray branches were scaly and barren. The tree was dying, for this is how they die—from the top down. The most important part of a tree is the roots. That is their heart and what connects them to the community of all living things. The only way to save the tree would be to chop it down and then from the stump new saplings would grow. But I had no axe.

Often the handyman would join me. He enjoyed smoking cigarillos and telling me stories of how things used to be in the house during its heyday of debauchery—the wild nights, lighting fires in the middle of the floor when the chimneys became too choked with soot. There were stories of dirty needles and broken bottles and women caught unaware—but then the lure of his television became too great and he would slink indoors with the others.

Once he was gone and once Mrs. B's light was out for the night, I would take my wig from its paper bag and put it on. The wig hair was black and long. I was on my way to Carla.

*

I needed practice before I gave myself over completely, before I offered myself up as the sacrificial crow. I went to the barber up the street and asked him to cut my hair. I needed it sleek so that it would fit better beneath the wig. The barber had fought in Viet Nam, was used to buzz cuts and folded newspapers. "You sure, girlie?"

Sure. Sure.

He gave me a perfect bob. "I love it," I said, shaking my head back and forth as he used a tiny broom to sweep the stray hairs from my shoulders. "May I use your bathroom?" I met his eyes in the mirror as I asked. He shrugged yes. "Where is it?"

"Back there," he said, hooking his thumb behind him. "Past the curtain."

The curtain was gingham, red and white. A tablecloth that someone had sewn into this other purpose. The bathroom was tidy, white. There was no can of air freshener; instead a book of matches on the back of the toilet served the purpose. He was a man, but he was not dirty. This comforted me.

As I washed my hands, I took in my new look. The cut was blunt, but not without style. The barber had done his best. I smiled. Nodded to myself.

I peeked out from behind the curtain: the shop was empty but for the barber. "Can you come here?"

"What?" he said.

"I need help," I said. He looked wary but came behind the curtain. I faced him, pulled him towards me by hooking a finger into the waistband of his trousers. "I owe you," I said. "For the cut." Then I kissed him. He fought me but I fought back and ended up giving him a blowjob in his tidy bathroom.

He cried afterwards. Said I had been pushy. Said he had buried his wife just a few weeks before and we had disgraced her.

I thought of the grackles as they mercilessly stormed the lawn in search of grubs. As they pecked away at the tomatoes, which my father had planted with fierce hopes of some delicious soup come September.

*

After many nights of surveillance, I saw the man I took to be Carla's pimp. Beneath the streetlights his skin was as pale as uncooked turnip. He continually scratched the inside of his left ear. He was unmistakable and would have been easy to pick out of a line up. "Hey," I called to him from up on the porch. "Wait up."

He kept walking—thinking I was not talking to him or possibly not hearing me. He might have a defect of hearing that required testing. I could talk to him about that, offer some suggestions for treatment. I pulled my wig down tight and took the stairs two at a time. I ran to catch him, wheezing with the smoke from my last cigarette, the thick August air.

"You," I said, grabbing the pimp by the arm. His skin was softer than expected, damp and soft as the lamb's ear growing in my garden back home.

"Get off me, motherfucker!" he said, turning, affecting a wrestling stance. He resembled Jared around the lips, the eyes. They might have been brothers.

"I'm off!" I said, hands in the air, stepping back.

"Shouldn't sneak up. Get yourself hurt." The pimp turned to go.

"I'm seeking employment," I said.

"Do you see 'Help Wanted' anywhere on me?" He faced me and stuck an index finger in his chest.

"I want to be one of your girls," I said, "I need protection." I held out my hand. "I'm Carla." I watched for any sign of hesitation or recognition of the name.

"Why are you messing with me?" he said and turned to go.

"I know what you did," I said, but he didn't hear me, finger already digging into left ear.

I waited in that doorway, my back against the same cool glass—her glass, her coolness. The pimp was not visible, but I knew he was there, watching me, just as he had watched Carla before me.

I was careful to keep a cigarette lit so that the one I awaited would see the burning ember, would know of my existence. The one I awaited would be older, but not too old. He would still be strong enough to overpower me if he needed to, if that was what he desired.

Traffic tapered off to one or two cars an hour, until after 2:30 when all went still. My wig was itchy and I was weary, so I left my spot, walked back toward the house when a car pulled up. "You like to party?" the man asked. I nodded. I had never gotten into a car with a stranger before and felt a thrill at the slip of his car's leather seats beneath my pale thighs as I pulled the door shut and sealed myself within the vehicle.

He drove out to where the abandoned factories stood sentinel. We parked near a building within which shoes were once made—shoes that traveled to New York, to Philadelphia, to Boston. Shoes for the feet of a young, bright country. Shoes for short life spans and limited incomes. Shoes for a simpler time.

"I'm Carla," I said.

He took my left hand in his own, small hand. He tugged me closer to him on the bench seat of his Chrysler Supreme. "All right," he said and opened the car door, exited, and pulled me out behind him.

He wore green Dickie work pants and a gray short sleeve shirt. His brown hair had been recently cut. He wore glasses. Biofocals. Boots, not shoes. White socks. I gathered all of the details of this man, Carla's killer. He was thin. He parted his hair on the side. He had a limp—slight, like a stutter.

He brought me to a door that led into the shoe factory. Carla was with me then, urging me to break free. *Run,* she said.

With that, I withdrew my hand from his and kicked off my shoes as I did. I ran, my bare toes gripping the rutted pavement, running as I had when I was a child and all that chased me was time. The killer pursued, the thud of his boots a heartbeat behind me until they trailed off to silence.

Then I was alone, a shoeless savior of the modern world. I stopped beneath a streetlight in a quiet neighborhood and took in the scene. There were no cars. The only sound was the stuttering love cries of the tree frogs. Above, there was not even the hint of a moon, just sky, murky, pond-like, with Carla, white and glowing, hanging like a shaved fingernail looking down upon me with gratitude, with love.

YOU DON'T NEED LOVE

The kitchen did nothing but look out onto the parking lot behind the Asian market. Sometimes there were crates of chicks next to the dumpster. If you opened the window you could hear the baby birds peeping, their flimsy claws scrabbling against the wood. But there wasn't anything to see, really, and now a man was dead and Junie was the only one living in the building.

The lesbian couple in the apartment below Junie moved out in late August leaving her alone on the second floor with only the old lady in the adjoining big house. It was April and the earth was thawing. The man had died in January and stayed cold enough through the winter that she could not smell him. It was not until the first extended stretch of warm days, daffodils blooming softly beneath the willow tree in the old lady's yard, that Junie smelled his unfortunate decomposition.

Festering, oozing, layering himself into dust beneath her.

All those nights she had lain in her bed listening to the wind push against the storm windows, wondering about what was next and feeling an unfurling excitement in her ribs. All those nights that she had reveled at being so far from home and all that was familiar to her. He had been there all those nights, dead.

Though there would have been some point when he wasn't actually dead. Presumably, he had died there below her. His last breath exhaling upward and through the floorboards and into her room. His last breath forming the shape of a cat and curling into the notch her knees made in sleep. His last breath a woman dressed in stars above her.

The police had questioned her about the man even though the coroner said he had died from too much drink. A body can't take all of that night after night. At some point the body breaks down, one of the officers said.

She felt the police were skeptical about her responses to their questions and that they held her responsible for the man's death. She wanted to assure them that she would not have simply left a body to rot below her. There were places back home, out in the skunk cabbage, deep in the forest, where you could put a body and no one would ever find it. Not here in this city, in these rented rooms below her.

She drank vodka as she spoke to the police. Shots and shots. The handsome one suggested she slow down. But the old lady's son was visiting and while Junie had never liked him, she agreed that he could stay with her for an hour or so while she sobered up. The police said they wouldn't leave until she said yes and so she said yes.

The old lady's son was 42 and malevolent. He was named Karl and had never been married and liked to lean up against his car and smoke cigarettes and bitch to Junie about his mother. She's a cunt, he liked to say, and she always has been. Junie had never heard anyone say the word out loud before. It sounded even uglier coming from his pale, crusty lips.

After the police left, she and Karl sat side by side on the couch drinking shots. The window was open and the sun broke through the clouds just as rain began to pour down.

I like the sound of rain, Karl said and took her hand in his. She wanted to let go of his hand and she did not want to let go. It might have been the only thing keeping her tethered to the room as her head felt balloon-like and swimmy. She was a vapor.

Karl pulled her onto his lap, her bottom resting between his thighs. He put his arm around her back and pushed her head down to his shoulder and said, there, there, now, a darling gesture he must have learned from his old cunty mother. Junie hadn't realized she was crying until he did that.

Karl stroked her back and held her other hand. She saw that his fingers were lovely, the nails clean and tapered. She didn't know what he did for work. She didn't need to know. She would not love him.

Junie believed that she could live in the box of her life by herself and so long as she had air and water and food, she would survive. You don't need love, she told herself in her bed at night lying above a man who was dead or dying beneath her floor, beneath her beating heart.

You do not need love, she said, and time will not stop. Time will not stop without it. Time is merciless.

ANOINTED

This was the guy who quoted Pygmalion, as if I was his diamond in the rough. And this was the guy who stood in the driveway, a real Gatsby, and spread out his arms and said, "This is my house," as if I was made holy there.

But his friend (the one renting the little house from him--the front house, the small house, the house that was once a post office where I had collected my mail on summer mornings, the box key shiny from the many fingers before mine, the postmaster in visor, waiting for the guests to arrive, the sun shallow across the lake) found him five days too late. And so he died. But I carried his mark.

It was in this smaller of the two houses, with bead board walls and those plastic curtains for doors, where it happened. It was in the house with Hank Williams on the turntable. It was in that house where he brought me behind the curtain and said my hair reminded him of riding in a boat before the thunder, when the static brings it all alive, forms a halo.

Then his dry lips anointed my forehead.

It would have been around now that he went into that other, bigger house—the back house, the veranda house, the death house—with a bottle, a coyote denning up somewhere. Pawing the ground in a circle, waiting for winter to end, curling around himself and looking up at the pockmarked sky, seeing the two of us on a boat near the island where blueberries grow and knowing how my hand would fit into his, silk on silk. And how, with the form of his lips a stigmata upon me, his eyes would shine down as I waited, away, far away, for sleep, gentle, gentle, for sleep.

ALLERGIC

We flew into Gatwick, not Heathrow like everyone said. Then we took the fast train into the city. While the bleak landscape flashed by, I pointed to the large bowls shrouded in metal. They were the size of buildings, sort of like silos but industrial, urban. What are they? Electricity or gas or something is what Blake said. I couldn't focus on what that meant. And then everything blurred and all I could see was Blake's reflection in the window, beaming back at me in the light of morning.

I was thinking of being there in England. Being on the tube. Saying, the tube. We'd talked about it so much late at night with candles lit as we sat cross-legged on the floor of our apartment. We'd talked about it so much that the trip had taken on its own persona. It had become its own thing.

When I thought the trip, I pictured a room I'd found in one of the old Seventeen magazines Luddy kept in a box under his bed. The room had pink walls and daisies and green chairs and a dressing table. It seemed the happiest room. And that's where I was, right there in that room.

Blake gazed out the window as we rocked with the motion of wheels on rail and ate his last bar of chocolate. I didn't know what he was thinking about.

Maybe that we had seen that guy from "Wings" getting on the plane back in Boston when they called first class and then we never saw him after that. Not even when we collected our luggage six hours later, wrinkled and smelling of canned air and stagnant breath. But he had been there on the plane with us as we hung suspended above the desperate sea.

Maybe that's what Blake was thinking about on the train into London, mouth rimmed with chocolate. About how someone had been on the plane with us and we'd never see him again except on television, in reruns.

*

It was not supposed to be hot in England. It was supposed to be cool and rainy, damp and dismal. It wasn't supposed to feel so American. But, of course, Blake hadn't bothered to tell me it would be hot and I was wearing a fleece sweatshirt I'd worn on the plane. I hated him, walking along in the new jeans he bought for the trip. It was his journey home and I was just along for the ride. We'd see the sights. Maybe we'd take the train up north and meet his mother. We'd drink in pubs. It would be great. It would be just like it always was. Me and Blake.

He was hungry so we stopped at a shop to buy some chocolate. I stayed outside, leaning against the brick wall with my massive pack still on. I didn't want to risk taking it off and then not being able to put it back on. I wanted to look like the type of girl who would own such a pack. Maybe people would mistake me for someone trekking across Europe. They wouldn't be able to see that I was poor and lonely and already homesick.

So I just stood there, wondering why I was here. Wondering why I wasn't appreciating everything that was around me.

Something had turned. Twisted. When I had seen them—Blake and Serge—on the kitchen floor at Thanksgiving doing what they were doing to each other. I tried to picture myself in Serge's spot with Blake touching me the way he was but the body I kept seeing was not mine. Then something fell away, the veil that Blake wore and I saw who he was and what he loved and it wasn't me.

Later that same night, curled up on myself in bed, I pulled the cover over my head and called Luddy. I told him all about what I had seen. About Blake and how his face melted into Serge's when they kissed. I told him how bad it made me feel. About how I wanted to be Serge.

"Why do you always do this to yourself?" Luddy said. "Can't you just be happy?" And I said that no, I couldn't. I could not be happy. But then he had to go because he heard Mother coming up the stairs in that soft way that she did when she wanted to overhear phone conversations. I told him not to say anything. I could hear the springs of his mattress squeak as he rolled over to hang up the phone and I wished I was there with him then, lying next to him and holding his hand. But I was alone in my bed and Blake was asleep in the next room.

Months had passed and Blake and I were in London-and I was in the red phone booth. My pack wouldn't fit so I had to take it off. I tried to dial home, to call Luddy or Mother or someone with a familiar voice but I couldn't figure out how to do it and there were too many colored fliers of ladies with their legs spread<orange, blue, red vaginas staring at me.

Blake, his face a pale moon of concern, knocked on the glass and said, "All right?"

I put my hand on the sticky glass and pushed the door open.

*

We got to the place. The buildings were all whitewashed. The street was white—buildings and buildings and the sun was beating on them and I hadn't slept on the plane. Instead, I drank free wine and ate the chocolates the attendants gave me and listened to Blake snort out his nose because he was allergic to chocolate. So the buildings were white and swimming around me. I told Blake we needed to find someplace to rest, fast.

He chose the cheapest place. Not a hostel. We didn't want a hostel because we wanted to stay together instead of being separated by sex. I didn't want to have to see Swedish girls strip down naked with no problem and me having to pull my bra out my sleeve. I didn't want anyone to see my sweaty American breasts.

Blake didn't want it either. Didn't want to be just with all men. That's what he said but that was only to be nice to me.

This place had its own bath and one double bed knocked up against the wall, right under the window. We would have to share and one of us would be blocked in, clinging to the wall like a spider.

Blake lay down on the bed and I took a bath. It was so hot that I opened up the windows onto the back courtyard and the surrounding buildings and then I soaked in the tub. I didn't mind the rust stains so much and when water dripped on me at first I didn't react until I realized that it was coming from the ceiling and beyond that I didn't know, just the ceiling is what I told myself. The ceiling, dingy. I let my head sink under the water and stayed like that.

I brought my head back out and gasped for air. I could hear Blake breathing in the other room, asleep. I closed my eyes and when I opened them I saw a man—hairy, dark, big eyebrows, belly—in the window across and he was looking at me. He was dressed but he had his penis in his hand. I yelled, "Blake" and he came to me. I tried to show him but the man was no longer there.

His penis was gone as well.

*

I woke up and it was still dark out. I couldn't get to my watch. And then I realized I was alone. Blake was gone.

He had disappeared. He did this back home where we lived, where we worked together.

It usually happened like this: we'd be in the mall and he'd go to the bathroom and not come out again for a while. And he would go off on his bike alone at night and go to the park where men were. It wasn't safe, I told him. You need to be careful, Blake, I would say. I never added , Because I love you.

And now he was out there and he had the key. I didn't even know where I would go if he didn't show up. I was locked in. Keyless.

My plan: I would signal to the penis man and have him get in touch with the front desk and have them let me out.

I couldn't get back to sleep so I ate some of Blake's chocolate. He was allergic to it anyway. He would be better off without it.

*

Blake came back to the room when it was almost morning. I told him about how I was locked in and what if he hadn't come back? Told him about my plan to flag down the penis guy. Didn't tell him that I'd eaten his chocolate and buried the wrappers in the trash. Didn't tell him that I hated him so much that I wished he would just die and leave me alone. We lay next to each other and he said, "Sorry. Sorry. I thought you had the key."

I said, "I think I'm allergic to you."

But Blake didn't hear me because he was snoring like a man would. Snoring like a man holding his penis and watching a girl in a tub. A tired girl, far from home.

*

Luddy used to ask me, "Why do you love Blake so? Why?"

And all I could say was this: His skin smells of coconuts. When I'm scared, he grabs my hand and squeezes it so that I feel safe. It feels like thunder rolling across my ribs when he makes me laugh.

But what I didn't ever say to Luddy was this: Once, I kissed Blake.

We were lying side by side on my bed, stinking of cigarettes from the club we'd been at all night. We were lying there laughing and making fun of the people we saw, like the woman who had lipstick on the outside of her lips. And the sad old guy who was hanging around the Eurotrash girls. We were laughing about them and then we stopped and Blake closed his eyes.

I raised myself up on one elbow and I looked at him. His eyelids so light and tender. His lips still smiling.

I kissed him then, lightly, lips on lips.

And he didn't say anything else, just this, "You have the softest lips."

*

I have pictures of pigeons swarming around Blake eating bits of food out of his hands. I have a picture someone took of the two of us in front of Buckingham Palace. I'm shielding my eyes in what looks like a salute but was really because it was so sunny and Blake has his hands in front of his crotch in the grape leaf pose.

I don't have any pictures of the last time I saw him. We were sitting in a bar at Gatwick waiting for my plane home. There was Blake eating chocolate, licking it off his fingers and stopping to blow his nose when the allergies kicked in. And me drinking a Bloody Mary, siphoning all of the vodka out of it and ordering another.

DISHES

We did the dishes rarely--once or twice a week. Mostly they were red tinged wineglasses or heavy blue glasses with crusty milk rims piled up easily and out of sight in the deep soapstone sink. I would lift them one by one and place them on the wooden countertop. Sometimes there would be mold and sometimes not. It depended on how long they'd been there, how hot it was outside. It depended on the closeness and direction of the sun. It was cosmic.

*

The apartment was the middle floor of a Victorian. Ours had been partly the original maid's quarters. Our kitchen was a sink and a pantry.

Our bathroom had small blue tiles on the floor, and once a dead mouse rotted underneath the claw foot tub.

The moldings, the built-ins, the place had it all. It even had two bedrooms but we used the second one as a den. Until he moved out and then it became my bedroom and the one we had shared became the bedroom of someone else. An other's room.

*

We could fit two low chairs and a small hibachi on the deck. To call it a deck is a stretch. It was more like a precarious overhang with railings.

I would sit out there and smoke, using the hibachi as an ashtray. The couple next door waved to me once. Pleased and envisioning my entrée into their clever, perfectly ordered lives, I smiled, waved. "Hey," he said, "Hey, so do you mind taking in that blanket you have hanging there? It's an eyesore." Eyesore this, motherfucker.

*

In the kitchen there was a table he made with green veneer on top and computer legs underneath. I got in trouble once for ironing on it. I had a sheet underneath but still veneer can come unstuck. It's the glue and the heat from the iron. Things come unstuck.

There was a gas stove, which could double as a heater if the power went out. Asphyxiation was an issue, though.

*

One summer the ceiling in the pantry was coated in tiny worms that plopped down on us. The landlord said they came from whole organic, unprocessed foods. Not my bleached floor then. She said not to worry about them that if they got in our food we would have more protein in our diet. ha ha. She said to put our food in jars. She said the worms would become moths.

And then what?

They turned into soft white wings, flittering around the pantry.

And then there were more worms.

I went wild with the worms and the moths. I threw out all of the food. I bought ball jars. I scrubbed everything.

Then they were gone.

I blamed the masseuse upstairs. I knew her food must have been organic, worm ridden and full of protein, ha ha. When I moved out I gave her the damn pencil cactus (it would not die no matter how we tried to kill it) as a form of gift torture. She thanked me.

*

The squirrels in the swatch of a yard would not put up with any shit. Give me your food. Right in your face. Give me your food, motherfucker.

*

Parking was a chore. I bumped a car once. And I mean bump--gently tiny rocking bump. I said nothing and got a notice that I was being sued for insurance for totaling some guy's Monte Carlo with my Civic. These things happen, my insurance agent said, that's why you should always call me first.

Give me your food.

Someone left notes on all of the cars, calling us on our imagined parking infractions. Taking up two spaces. Parked too close to the curb. Parked too far away from the curb.

Once there was a neighborhood meeting about the notes. We were not in attendance.

*

We brought his old clothes, the ones that would be otherwise left behind, in three black garbage bags to the Salvation Army. I wore a pair of his dress pants from eighth grade that he let me keep. Afterwards we lay side by side in the bed that was no longer ours. Not ours together. We watched the light move behind the blinds, changing from day to evening to night.

When he left I washed the dishes. A wineglass, a blue glass, two coffee mugs. The sink was clean and empty.

THE
WHITE
BUTTON

In December the snow was so deep that deer knocked over the birdfeeder and denuded the shrubs at the front of Eve's house, eating even the rhododendron leaves, all other forms of nourishment lost to them, covered over with white.

Hesitant sun poked through the evergreens and spiked the snowy yard that morning. It was mild. In the 30s. Earlier she heard footsteps squeaking up the snow covered drive—a man come to invade her house and kill her. But when she got up to check she found the dog in the hallway, his nails scratching against the tile from his dreaming movement.

Outside there was no man, but trees. Beyond the trees there were roofs, whcih throughout the region had fallen prey to ice dams. The eaves, heavy with ice and snow from rapid thaws and freezes and snows, were dammed so that behind them icy water backed up onto the roof and threatened to seep through into the house proper.

Ceilings caved in. Walls leaked. Nasty business.

Eve noticed the first drips in the window casings in the upstairs bedrooms. Soon the walls beaded and splotched. Her house was sweating on the inside.

She pawed through the tiny local phone book and settled on Fixit General Contractors. A man answered. "Talbot," he said. She understood this was his name.

She spoke, breathless. Something weird was happening with her house. Water seemed to be coming from everywhere. Through her walls. Like a sign from God. Or the Virgin Mary. One of the stains might actually be in the shape of the Virgin Fucking Mary. She couldn't tell for sure. Oh god, she needed help. Help. Could someone help? Please? She was a woman alone in these wild mountains. She needed help. Help me, goddamn it!

"I'll be out this afternoon," he said.

"I need you now." In response, she heard him shuffling papers on a desk or table. Clearing his throat. The air moved in and out of his nose with precision. "The water is everywhere."

"I'll be there after lunch," he said and hung up. Eve would have been infuriated if she hadn't been so grateful. All she needed to do was wait until after lunch.

*

When Talbot arrived, Eve was standing in the driveway. She wore a bright orange down vest over a black sweater and jeans. Her dog's leash rested in one hand and a toilet plunger in the other. "Thank god you're here," she said as he got out of his truck.

He nodded and eyed the roof. Icicles hung down several feet and a good foot of snow was backed up. It was a mess. "I'll just get my ladder," he said.

"What should I do?" Eve said. She twirled the toilet plunger in her hand as if it were an umbrella. The dog sank down and chewed on the crusty snow.

"Might as well go inside and wait. It's going to take me a while."

Each time he descended the ladder, she was there gawking at him through the front window, plunger in hand. Later when they knew each other better he asked her about the plunger. "I don't own a baseball bat," she said.

"So you were going to plunge my face off if I tried anything funny?" he asked.

"You got it."

But he hadn't tried anything funny. Instead he went about his work and thought about her. It wasn't that she was so pretty. She was a good looking woman, sure. Strong jaw, clear eyes. But there were plenty of good looking women in the world. Hell, they even had some good looking women born and bred right there in the North Country.

He liked women, but in a fearful way. Partly because he was shy, but mostly because of his secret. Talbot still slept with a pacifier. He'd never been able to give it up and the only other person who knew his secret was his mother and she took this secret to her grave, God bless her.

This secret had kept him from doing just about everything he'd ever wanted to do—go to college, find a nice wife, have kids. None of it had happened because he could not bear to give up his pacifier. He'd sooner have died. And since he couldn't give it up, he couldn't foresee how he could ever sleep in a room with another human being. Just the thought of it filled him with a shame so blistering that his cheeks would redden and his hands shake. And the shame made him crave the nipple—so supple and comforting against his tongue. He didn't think there was anything else in the world that could make him feel so satisfied.

*

Eve ended up at the lake because it seemed to her there was nowhere else to go. Rather, there was nowhere else she could imagine herself being without wanting to peel her skin off strip by strip. It had been a childhood vacation spot. A place of memories—not necessarily happy, but not sad either. It was this middle ground she sought after Chet left her.

The last time she'd seen him was at the reflecting pool at the Christian Science Center. It was early June and stifling. Grimy children ran in and out of the fountain—some in bathing suits, some in shorts and t-shirts, others in underwear. Their weary parents sat on the sidelines, out of the spray, grateful for a chance to get their kids cooled off.

Eve waited for Chet on one of the stone benches. Above the traffic noise of Huntington Ave and Mass Ave and Boylston, she heard the whine of his motorcycle. He was going fast and he knew she would know he was and that it would irritate her. She gritted her teeth.

He was free to do whatever he wanted now. They were no longer together. She'd made that clear. Even though he was the one physically leaving—taking off cross-country on his bike—she was the one who left. Or at least that's what she told herself. And this was the last good bye. He'd already moved all of his shit into the basement of his sister's house in Framingham and now all that was left was for him to turn over the key to her condo.

He snuck up behind her, sweaty palms covering her eyes. "Ha, ha," Eve said. He slid his hands away from her eyes and she smelled the lingering tobacco and motor oil from his skin and something else: the unique himness of him.

She was making a mistake.

He straddled the bench and sat facing her profile. He slipped the key into her hand. "You could have mailed it," she said, turning the key over and over in her palm with the flick of her fingers.

He stood and took her by the hand and pulled her up next to him and then he bent her over backward and kissed her in a dramatic, winning way. He always had loved an audience. The kiss lingered and he reached a hand down the waistband of her thin cotton skirt and snapped the elastic of her underpants.

And then all that was left was the whine of his bike over the traffic. It was only later as she waited alone for the #39 bus that she realized he'd not said a word.

So she was at the lake and he was gone. She pictured him traveling west, his bike blazing past fields of sunflowers, tall grass, gazelles, and prairie dogs.

*

Before there was such a thing as online shopping, Talbot had to travel for his pacifiers. He had driven up to 150 miles to cover his tracks and always he ended up buying more than just the pacifier—he'd get diapers or a few toys as well, which he ended up leaving the bag behind in a shopping cart, hoping some needy parent would find them.

Sure he had tried to quit, but always this ended in sleep deprivation and wild mood swings. He had toyed with the idea of hypnosis or something like that, but how could he do it when he'd have to tell the person hypnotizing him what he wanted to give up?

It seemed easier, then, to just carry on as he was and to resign himself to the fact that this was his life and that he would go out the way he came in, alone.

But then there was the worry. What if he died suddenly or what if he went mad or was paralyzed and needed to be cared for? People would enter his home, invade his sanctuary. He would be discovered. His secret found out.

*

Eve sold her condo in Jamaica Plain, put most of her belongings in storage, bought a little four-season cottage on the lake sight unseen and headed north, unsure of who and what she would find there. She remembered people from her childhood summers. She remembered Francesca, who had a moustache and sold penny candy in her store and how Eve was mesmerized by her, so much so that her mother had to warn her not to stare. "There'll be no treats for you if you gawk at that poor woman," Eve's mother said.

Of course, as an adult she ached for Francesca. Why had she not bleached the thing? Waxed it? Eve herself knew how easy it was to hide one's womanly deformities. And whenever she was lax about her grooming, she always had Chet to remind her, plucking at the stray black hairs growing up from her nipples.

The shame.

Men knew no such shame. She was convinced of this. All of their hair, all of their burps and farts and blood and fat, all of their many excretions, were just as they were meant to be.

Oh sure, they had erections, but these were easily covered over and dealt with. When had a man ever had to worry about blood in his underpants or, heaven forbid, seeping through the crotch of his white capris? When?

Up north she would be shameless. She would live alone in her small house and let the hair around her nipples flourish. It was a new beginning.

*

The house came furnished—a hodge-podge of maple furniture from the 50s. It would do. The view was, as promised, spectacular—mountains, sky, water. In the summer she would practice yoga on the dock as the sun rose and drink a glass of wine in that same spot at sunset.

It was electric baseboard heat, which would be expensive, but she had savings enough left over from her condo and she was sure she'd find a job. Teaching or something. Maybe she could write ads for a local paper? She hadn't really thought it all through, but something would come along. Until then, she would settle into her house and wait for winter. It was September when she moved in. Chet had been gone for 63 days.

Never mind.

September was golden and red and burning orange. It was warm afternoons and chilly nights. However, September did not prepare her for December. The sun behind the mountains by 4. The dark mornings.

She had never known such silence—so quiet you could hear the ice groan as it froze. So quiet you could hear the cold settling onto the branches and filling up the cracks in the clapboards of the house. So quiet.

*

The dog showed up on Halloween. Eve put out a jack o'lantern and bought candy, but no children showed up. Before she went to bed that night she stepped outside to blow out the candle in the pumpkin when she noticed a dog sitting outside of the range of the porch light. He looked to be a shepherd mix. A sturdy dog, but skinny, sickly, stray. Normally she would have been terrified of such a creature, remembering any number of large dogs which chased her and her sister as children, but she craved.

She had always considered herself a loner when she lived in the city, but now this, this was really being alone and she didn't like it. The wind was not enough. "I need more," she surprised herself by saying out loud one night as she lay in the dark waiting for sleep. "More, more." Repeating made it prayer rather than desperate plea in the darkness. More, more.

She bent and blew out the candle and met the dog's gaze. "You might as well come in, then," she said. He didn't move. Was she dreaming him?

"Come," she said and thinking better of it, "Come, boy," unsure of his sex. She opened the door and showed him the way in with the swoop of her arm. He stood. She stepped over the threshold and then he did come trotting in, falling in a heap on the doormat, lifting his head only to lap some water and devour the can of tuna she put out for him. More, more.

*

He told her that the walls would need work. "Might need to replace the drywall." Eve nodded, unsure whether this was true or not. She had never paid much attention to things—how they were constructed. That was Chet's job. He was the one who walked through her condo with the inspector before she signed the papers. She hadn't even known an inspection was necessary. "It's just something you've got to do, Babe," Chet said. And so she had.

She thought of him on his bike, rolling on, the wheel spinning into oblivion, as she nodded. She wanted to send him a message so that he might send one back and tell her what to do. "What do you think I should do?" she asked Talbot.

"Water can do a lot of damage," he said, ominously. Eve nodded. She had heard from Chet—postcards forwarded to her from her old address. They were all from southern states, not what she expected. They were signed only with his name, no love or miss you. Just Chet. She got the feeling he wrote the same thing on all of the postcards he sent and he knew she would know that. It was a chastisement.

She had ridden on the back of Chet's bike down to Providence once, weaving in and out of traffic on 93. On the way down, she'd been tense, her hands bunched into fists around his waist. But on the way home she'd been so tired that she fell asleep for a few minutes, her body trusting that he would keep them moving forward. She had been drifting, the air flying past and around her helmet, her body suspended—it was that place between life and death. An out of body experience. Had she seen light? When she woke she realized with horror that she could have killed them—leaned this way, fallen that way. But they had not died.

"Let's fix the walls," she said. Talbot nodded. She had made the right decision.

*

Talbot owned two bi-planes, each built from a kit. One of the planes he flew regularly in the summer; the other—he would tell his passengers once they were well above the ground—was at the bottom of the lake. Ha. Ha.

As a child Talbot jumped off cliffs, from tree limbs, arms and legs flailing from bridges into rivers below. There was something about the way his body connected with air. He had sky dived the one time and then decided to get his pilot's license, which is what led to the biplanes.

When he was in the air, his secret was forgotten. And then there was the precious release when the pontoons hit the water, glided briefly, made contact. The landing, the takeoff, those were the moments of reaching the sublime, when he imagined a white button in the back of his brain shattering and splintering into exquisite release. He was young again, his father throwing him over and over into the air, the sun shifting and shadowing his father from behind. He had trust that he would not fall.

*

January was black and snow and then there was February—darkness leading to darkness leading to blue sparkles at noon. She had never really known winter before this. "Is every winter this way?" she asked Talbot. He was there several times a week, fixing her walls, her ceilings, projects that seemed to be taking longer than they should, but she was glad. He filled up the time between morning and night.

"What way?" he asked. He had a few corny jokes and some long, droll stories about local people she did not know but other than that she found him difficult to converse with.

"So fucking cold," she said. She hadn't had opportunity to swear much since Chet left. It felt good and she was testing the water to see how he would react.

"I suppose," he said. She leaned in the doorway of the room he was working on—her spare bedroom—and lifted her right foot up and hooked it behind her left leg. Had she offended him?

"I'll take you up in my plane this summer if you like." His offer drifted out in the air between them, purple and strange. She wasn't sure what to say. It implied their knowing each other would extend beyond this season—that outside of his working for her, they would meet and enjoy time together.

He had not turned from his work but had stopped hammering, waiting—hovering in anticipation—for her to say something. She opened her mouth, but could not speak. She breathed in, out. He took up hammering.

*

One month before Chet left, he asked her to meet him at his work. He took her into South Boston, down to the loading docks. They'd been there before when they first met. He brought her over the chain link and onto a cement slab one night—they had a picnic, watched the murky water shiver as they drank wine right from the bottle. She'd been scared of climbing the fence, disobeying the warnings. They were trespassing. Later in their relationship, he'd come to mock her fear, always edging her forward until her toes were in space and she was falling off a cliff. And forward she would move, never wanting him to think she was not worthy of him, flawed and fearful though she was.

He led her back to that spot. It was a muggy evening in May, and still light. "Remember this?" he said, grabbing two fistfuls of fence.

"Sure," she said.

He dug a foot in and started to climb. "Come on," he said.

"I don't want to."

"Don't be that way." He hoisted himself up another foot. "Come with me."

Eve crossed her arms, looked around to make sure no one saw them. She thought she might scale the fence, give in to his goading one last time. Show him that she was worthy. In the distance she heard laughter, horns honking. A breeze brought in a waft of rotting fish, kelp. Chet pulled himself up and over the fence, stood on the other side of it facing her. She didn't move. Noted, instead, that his face was the fearful one. If she didn't follow him, who was he then?

"Aren't you coming?" he said.

*

After Talbot made his offer and could not take it back, the idea grew so large in his mind that he could think of nothing but taking Eve up in his plane. Before sleep he ran through the movie of how he would land near her dock and take her by surprise while she was sunbathing.

She would wrap a towel around her hips like a sarong and allow him to attach the belts around her when she sat in the passenger seat. He imagined the hot smoothness of her skin beneath his fingers as they glided over it.

He would see the water dividing beneath them as they took off, the sun shooting through the windows. She would turn and smile.

Talbot would point out the mountains on the horizon, the dark center, leading to the russet edges of the tannin-laced water. The dark green of the trees and the paler, more vibrant green of the fields. The orange sail on a catamaran, small now and far away.

He would say, Do you love it up here?

Yes.

Back on the ground, he would help her out of the plane and she would suspend in his arms, her mouth reaching for his. And when she kissed him, her tongue would linger on his tongue and he would suck on it so gently that she would not even notice he'd done it. Everything would fall away then, fall backwards and upwards. The gentle suckling. The white button opening up.

*

It was spring. Nearly a year since Chet had left. Talbot made a joke about a sunken plane. She did not react. She heard the whine of the plane engines, felt the vibration of air over wings.

Instead of seeing mountains and sky and water from the plane window, Eve saw herself turning from the chain link fence and walking back along the pier as streetlights flickered on in the distance. Behind her she heard the jingle of Chet scaling the fence, the slap of the soles of his Converse as he ran in the opposite direction.

The sky above her was a prairie divided by road. Hot black tarmac, a wheel pushing forward.

LET ME GO

The mothers were starving, except for those who did not smoke. They ate well and were plumper. Those who did not smoke, vacationed in Switzerland, brought home fine chocolate that tasted vaguely sour and masticated.

It was unclear whether their husbands liked them this way, plumper, but one of the smoking mothers found one of the non-smoking mothers in bed with her husband.

They were in adjoining hotel rooms, away for a couple's weekend, and had indulged in too many martinis at the bar. She had gone for cigarettes and come back to find them, side by side, turned toward each other. His hand on her hip, their faces this close. Her husband was shorter than the plump wife. He was muscle and sinew, small hands, bitten nails.

She said nothing. Left the room. Stood by the glittering pool with her cigarettes, smoking, breathing in chlorinated air, thinking of her thinness.

Oh what a glorious life it had been. What a glorious globe of a life.

If she could paint this life she would paint it in a circle with a sun and moon and sun and a moon, all rising and setting and rising. And beneath that a blue sky and clouds and stars. And below that grass as green as a turtle leg and deep water and a field of poppies.

Sunflowers everywhere. Just everywhere.

She would paint herself in the middle, lying in a borrowed hospital bed on Easter Sunday waiting to die. She would paint her youngest daughter next to the bed, holding her hand, telling her it was okay to go now.

It's time. It's time.

How to capture the desperation on her daughter's face? Somewhere between fear and desire. Somewhere between pushing away and pulling in.

The face said, Let me go. Let me go.

WASH,
DRY,
FOLD

Phyllis ran the counter at a dry cleaner three days a week. Other days she did odd jobs. Walked dogs. Brought meals to shut ins. That sort of thing. But the dry cleaner was her main employer. She processed orders, delivered laundered clothing back to its owners, answered the phone, made change for the washers and dryers. It was quick, tidy work. She enjoyed being on her feet and scanning the rack of clothing as it spun. She relished the crisp odor of starch. She was friendly with the customers, allowed them to feel heard when they bitched about stains and missing buttons.

Often, a man named Greg phoned the dry cleaners and when he did, Phyllis spoke with him briefly and after he hung up, five minutes later, Greg would call again and attempt to resume the conversation. They were in the same network on Facebook—Manchester, NH. "I liked your profile," Greg said when she questioned him about why he had started messaging her, the messages then leading to lengthy phone calls.

"What about my profile?" Phyllis asked, intrigued. She hoped he liked her favorite quote:

If you live to be a hundred, I want to live to be a hundred minus one day so I never have to live without you.

—A. A. Milne

"You have high-brow taste in television," Greg said. "I thought you might be classy." She didn't really watch television. She checked out video tapes and DVDs from the library—most of them British shows from *PBS: The Black Adder. Are You Being Served?*

She lay on her bed with the phone up snug to her ear during this particular conversation and her room seemed smaller to her after he said this. She saw the light seeping around the edges of her light blocking shades. The way her double bed didn't seem big enough when she was in it alone. The sadness of her clothes folded neatly on her chair. She should have been untidy. She should have left her drawers ajar. If she smoked, she would have seemed more interesting, maybe. If her books were more intellectual.

Her apartment was three rooms. Kitchen/living space, bathroom, and this, her bedroom. Windows looked out onto the parking lot. Many young professionals lived in the building. It had seemed the perfect spot after her divorce, but now with this exciting young man in her life it felt dowdy.

From Greg's profile she learned that he enjoyed travel, Second Life, and foreign films. He listed his job as Professional Dreamer. His favorite quote:

The ladder of success is best climbed by stepping on the rungs of opportunity.

—Ayn Rand

But there was more to why Greg contacted her. He wanted. He wanted her, he said, to help him, please. His mother was six feet tall. She had never cut her hair. Would Phyllis please come and wash and dry it? Run a comb through it? Brush it? His mother had such beautiful hair. Auburn or strawberry blonde. He wasn't sure the color exactly as it changed in the light. It changed with the years.

Phyllis said she would think about it, but Greg pushed to know when Phyllis would make her decision.

Soon, she said.

In her quiet moments, Phyllis composed an image of Greg's tall mother. Her loose hair. The ruddiness of her cheeks. The coarseness of her nipples from overuse. A wide, pale belly. A thicket of pubic hair.

But why had she assumed the woman would be naked? Less an assumption and more of a wish: The woman would be naked. Phyllis would enter the wide-plank, wood-floored kitchen and find the woman sitting on a hard-backed wooden chair, once painted red and now chipping. No cloth on the table, no dishes in the sink.

"My son brought you," the woman would say. She would stand then and turn, look back at Phyllis over her shoulder and then. And then. And then, Phyllis would see all of her beauty. "Come," the woman would say. And Phyllis would follow.

＊

Greg's dream was to produce a video called "Perfections/Imperfections." The setting would be a strip club in Vegas. On one side of the club would be the naked imperfections: the legless, the flippered, the obese. The blind. The pregnant.

And on the other side, the buff, the blonde, the beautiful. No stretch marks. No dimpled asses.

Customers would start out on the imperfections and after they had had their fill, move over to the perfections side to cleanse the palate, if you will.

And what of Phyllis? He had only her profile photograph to go on.

Which side was she? She wasn't a perfection, but then she wasn't exactly an imperfection either. He gazed at her Facebook profile photo. She appeared to have good hair. Thick, curly, long. Her eyes were washed out and verging on hopeless. She might have had a few small acne scars on her cheeks concealed not so well with makeup. Her nose seemed knocked off-kilter. Oh, he didn't know. There was a lot, he supposed, that made her an imperfection.

Most importantly, she was dreamless, or at least this was what he gathered when he asked her what her hopes were.

"I'm not sure," Phyllis said. Too quickly. She didn't have any hopes, no dreams, but he knew that already. And this was a fatal flaw, making her the ultimate imperfection. All of the perfections had hopes and dreams; they were stripping their way through grad school in order to get their PhDs or they were in law school. They wanted a better life for their families. They would buy their mother a house. They would make sure their own kids never wanted for anything.

While the imperfections wanted little. They were dreamless. They were passing time.

*

Greg's mother left when he was nine. Gone. Packed up. Drove away. Left her dental practice. Left her piano. Left her sons and her husband. Gone, gone, gone.

Where did she go? West in her Honda Accord. She sent postcards from Glacier National Park where she summered and from Seattle where she wintered. "I sleep in my car," the summer postcards said, "and during the day, I hike."

She had seen a grizzly. In Yellowstone, she had seen wolves.

"I am happy," her postcards said. "Please do not miss me, because I do not miss you," the cards said.

Love,

Mom.

*

Phyllis said yes to Greg. "I will wash your mother's hair," she said and he hung up, then called back in three minutes. "I'm sorry I hung up on you," he said. "I got excited."

*

Of course, Greg went in search of his mother. When he was nineteen, he borrowed money from his father and bought a small truck. "I'm going to get mom," he told his dad. "I will bring her home."

Greg's father wasn't sure he wanted his wife back. Life was simpler without her. There was dust under the bed. He liked it there.

*

Phyllis agreed to meet Greg on a Thursday. The rendezvous was to take place outside the dry cleaner. Though he had never seen Phyllis but for her photograph, Greg said he would know her. "I feel you," Greg said.

What was his mother's name?

Madeline.

Maddy?

No. She prefers you use her full name, please.

The day was hazy. Phyllis huddled beneath the awning, staring out across the parking lot. A few cars dotted the landscape. It was 7:30 AM and none of the other shops were open yet. The supermarket opened at nine, but the dollar store didn't open until 10 and Mike's Subs at 10:30. The dry cleaner was open, though. Jeanie was working the counter. She chatted with Phyllis when she stepped out for a smoke but seemed uninterested in why Phyllis was there on her day off.

At five minutes past rendezvous time, she wondered if he would show up at all. She watched as a red SUV pulled into the lot. She hadn't expected him to drive a vehicle like that. The car circled in front of the supermarket and then raced past her. The driver was a teenage boy. Not him. Greg was a man.

She shouldn't have said yes. She turned to check her face in the reflection of the window. She saw Jeannie leaning against a broom, staring up at the morning news on the television. There was a car accident on the screen. A medivac helicopter. Perhaps Greg was involved.

She returned her attention to her reflection. She saw him, then, walking across the parking lot. A baseball cap obscured his face in shadow. She turned to face him as he approached. He raised his hand in a wave.

*

Greg had an old photo of his mother taken just before she left home. She crouched awkwardly in their garden, planting impatiens. Her hands were bare and covered in dirt and she laughed as she turned to the camera. Her teeth were straight, barely any space between them to slide a piece of floss. The edges of the teeth were not flattened, rather slightly pointed. Predatory teeth. He would know her when he saw her. He would get her to smile and look for the sharpness.

Greg found his mother in West Glacier. It hadn't been difficult. It seemed everyone who worked in the park knew her, knew of her. She was something of a renegade. "She's had her run ins," one of the rangers told him, "But Maddy's good people." The ranger told him he'd find his mother's car in the parking lot of the general store near the campground. "She sleeps in her car," he said, "so either late night or early morning, she'll be there."

He found her car—a newer Accord than the one she'd left home in—

and waited beside it, hunched down, squatting on his heels. Where had she gotten the money for a new car? Probably his father had a hand in it. For a while Greg had suspected that his father was sending her money; this money kept her away from them, kept her living this transient lifestyle.

Greg cupped a hand up to the glass and peered through the windows. The backseat was made up as a bed with a sleeping bag and pillow. The front passenger side held a plastic bin filled with papers—cards, bank statements, scribbles on loose leaf. Folks passing by eyeballed him like he was a criminal. "I'm waiting for my mother," he yelled after they passed, when no one was around to hear him.

By nightfall, she had not appeared, so he climbed into the cab of his truck to wait. He kept the window cracked open so he would hear her approach. He awoke in the night. His neck ached from how it had lain to the side on the seat back. He looked to his mother's car parked next to his. He saw the back of her head against the window. She was reading in the light of a lantern. She turned slightly and he saw her in profile. Yes. Yes, that was his mother.

He yearned to reach a hand out and touch her wiry hair. Mama, he thought. It wasn't what he had called her as a boy. She was Mom. But in his mind he heard Mama again and again, growing louder, more panicky.

Greg fumbled with his keys in the ignition. He started the truck and drove straight out of the parking lot without turning on his lights. It wasn't until he was miles away on a stretch of road dangerous for the free-range cattle that he turned on his lights again. There along the side of the road a dozen pairs of eyes were illuminated. Cows and their calves, sleeping, chewing. He slowed as he passed them, reverent. He drove on and on until the voice in his head quieted. Until he was away from the pull of her.

*

Greg's body was slight. His hair, red. How had he such a tall mother? But maybe the woman wasn't his mother. Maybe she wasn't six feet tall. Maybe it was all a lie. She should not have agreed to meet him.

"You came," she said, finally, after the silence of the two of them standing face-to-face became too much. Gone was the comfort of the computer screen, the ease of the phone.

"We should go," Greg said. She noted that his hands and forearms were tanned and freckled. That his sneakers were cleanly white. She was comforted then that he was okay. And she would simply wash his mother's hair and that would be the end of it. She could do that. She could offer such kindness.

"Yes," she said, "let's."

*

The woman was bedridden. The mother. Maddy. Madeline. Her eyes were aware, showed gratitude, as Phyllis ran a comb through her drying hair. It had been a challenge to wash it. Phyllis had had to get in the tub with her and cradle the woman in between her legs as though she were giving birth to her. As if their embrace was anything other than out of utility. It was not the scene Phyllis had expected after all. There was nothing of the erotic she had anticipated, had craved.

The woman was aged. Her long hair was glorious but wiry. Her teeth, sharp. Greg had demurely left Phyllis to her work.

She felt for the woman. How to end up here living in a one-bedroom apartment with her son? He slept on the couch, he said. He made a point of saying.

Phyllis had answered Greg's call, this calling. She felt righteous and clean for serving this woman, but she could not do it again. She felt she had driven out her uglier thoughts. The ones involving her and the woman and their hands.

The air in the bedroom was overheated. Simply, Phyllis could not breathe. She looked out through the vast rectangle of the window. Beyond was the pale sky. Beyond that the stars and moon. Beyond and beyond and beyond this room there was air. This woman would die here. Phyllis knew that. She did not want to be there when it happened. She would satisfy herself that she had left this woman clean. It was enough.

*

Greg's mother wrote to him after he left Montana.

I waited for you. I stayed up all night. I was going to tell you about the huckleberries and where to find the best of them. You would have to share them with the bears, though, and so you might get eaten. But you drove away without even saying hello. Please do not miss me, because I do not miss you.

Love,

Mom.

PREY

There is not a great deal of light.

She lives at the bottom of a hill, in a valley of sorts. The sun goes down early. In the summer, it is behind the three big oak trees by 5PM. Without this light is a depression or an excuse to have cocktails earlier and earlier. By December, the glasses and ice were coming out at 3:59PM in anticipation of 4PM and darkness.

She remembered smoking on a stairwell, watching as rain fell somewhere in the distance. Rain sliced down, but sliced gently. Glasgow in December with the rain whispering down, the gray-light, white cloud sky, the three seconds of sunlight each day.

Not so different from where she was then, in this dark, wet place called home. Living in a bog, spongy earthed, sodden. A bog is like a swamp but not. From a lake, comes a meadow, comes a forest. There is a natural progression to these things. In one part of the forest on their walk is a sort of meadow filled with saplings. Soon, he tells her, this will be a forest.

There is also a stream they pass over. Dark, rocky, brooding. She is scared to walk there because it is near the dump and she fears that animals are nearby, searching for food, for prey. And she knows that if you get in the way of that, you are in trouble.

In this bog, there are toads, moss, and spiders, everywhere. The spiders invaded in May and stuck. Daddy Longlegs clung to the clapboards like starfish. The webs of lesser spiders in every windowsill. At first she thought that each week she would need to whisk them out with her broom, but as summer progressed and the rain fell and fell, it became an every day search.

The spiders, the ants, the slugs were everywhere. But there were also the fireflies, flicking on here and there in the edges of the forest on hot June nights. And there were also the dragonflies, high and higher in the dusk-light looking for the last mosquitoes before the bats came out and everyone hid.

*

Everyone hid when the bats came out. Afraid of claws tangled in hair, afraid of rabies dripping down. Afraid of their mousey, doggy faces that could be sweet but were ugly, but were mute. Their pointy ears, frisking, twitching.

Once there was a girl who poked a bat on the sidewalk with a stick. It was daylight, the creature desperate and dying on the hot ground. She poked it once, twice and its pink mouth opened revealing white pirrahana teeth. She flicked the thing onto the grass with her stick. On its back it pushed with its elbows until it managed to turn over but still could not fly. It edged across the grass to the shadows.

The bat is more scared of you than you are of it, the mother said. The bat is a helpful creature. It eats insects. Remove it safely. Do not kill it.

But she wanted it dead, wanted it gone. Those teeth. The furry ears, not benevolent. The blind eyes, the chalky squeak.

*

The sound of the hawk when he is hunting is almost a squeak but more like a squeal or a scream. The sound of the owl at night. One long and two short. One long and two short. Almost like a huffing sound.

The huffing sound of a bear. Didn't know if she had actually heard it before. With her sister, in the woods once when she pushed back a branch near the pump house and heard a huff, huff. Then ran. Down the hill, through the branches. Back home.

Of course, you should not run, they say. This makes the predatory instinct kick in. You are fleeing. You are prey.

*

The light drops through in chunks now. Through the heavy pine trees and onto the spongy ground. They could cut cubes out of the forest floor and make a sod house. Could live in their backyard in their very own sod house and could burn the sod in their very own sod house fireplace. They would likely be safe there.

ZEUS.
ZEUS?

Once there had been a beaver pond at the end of the street, but men from the highway department broke up the dam because it flooded the road during the spring rains. Now it was a plot of tall grass, gone white in the first frost. Beyond the grass, the road. Beyond that, trees and trees.

It is said that 80% of this state is forest.

The loggers arrived earlier than we expected, before the rain left its rhinestone trails on the window glass. Les said that the big one was in charge and that the other, smaller one seemed like he'd acquainted himself with one too many drug in his life. After coffee, the smaller one stamped out his cigarette in the dry leaves, while the big one climbed into the bucket of the crane, riding up to the top of the dead pine.

The chipper sat in the drive, waiting to be fed. The truck had a steel cover over its cab for when the tree parts fell—they often landed on it, on the steel. The machines tore at the moss on the side of the house.

The falling trees. How they fell. I knew that they were not really dead just from the cutting—not until their stumps are torn out of the ground. Then they would die.

I was told that we were cutting them to make way for the other trees, so that they would not be crowded. When I objected, Les called them a renewable resource. Said that even the native Americans cut down trees.

Why?

To build canoes.

We would not be building canoes.

I sat on our unmade bed, away from the window as I did not wish to see the trees as they were dismembered and sliced down to the stub.

I'd gotten up the night before and watched the oak out front in the moonlight. How still. Les slept on, unaware of the leaves and thin branches holding it all together. How the roots pull through the ground seeking others, water, air.

Later, the lost oaks smelled of vomit, the pines of unforgotten nights, the birches of the day I was born. Our yard waited in the fog of the oncoming chill. Come summer, suckers would grow up green and hopeful from the stumps. I heard my neighbor call out for her lost dog over and over in the distance, "Zeus. Zeus?"

HAVE YOU SEEN US?

Sylvie was out there again, green jacket flickering through the bare trees at the end of the driveway. Then the red and blue of her two boys, spilling in and out of the mud, down around the roots of the pines and birches that made up the culvert in the circle at the end of the cul de sac where they lived. The culvert was not meant to be played in, rather it served a purpose as part of the drainage system—a natural ditch which led underground and into a small brook at the edge of Maggie's lawn; a lawn speckled with crusty remnants of a late autumn snow storm.

Sneaking looks out her window, Maggie could tell from Sylvie's body language—a slight turn, a glimpse over her shoulder—that she wanted to meet eyes and give a wave. But if she allowed herself this eye meet, this wave back, Maggie knew that Sylvie would grab the boys and drag them to her door and then she would be trapped. There was too much work. And she was behind, dammit, because of Sylvie and her endless bonding and her tedious worry.

Maggie got up from her desk chair and tugged her heavy tab curtains shut, leaving only a crack through which she could see Sylvie and the boys. She sat back and examined the light chipping in, felt more than heard the computer hard drive whining, and wondered why they insisted on playing in the culvert. It was like they did it on purpose, to piss her off.

The boys could have played anywhere else on the slow, wide street. They could have played with the Franklin's Bernese mountain dog, Trixi, always tied up outside, barking, barking, barking. Maggie often stopped to pet her when she took her early morning walk through the neighborhood, down the street and up around the nature trail which circled the subdivision.

The boys could have ridden bikes up and down the Marshfield's winding driveway, leading up to their house—the only modern, split-level on the street of close-faced, New England capes, colonials and saltboxes.

They could have played at the basketball hoop, set up to the side of the Johnson's three-car garage two houses down from Maggie's. The sound of the ball tanging off the pavement wouldn't even have reached her where she sat avoiding the work she was paid to do—online auction description writing—a task she believed so arcane that only a few, like herself, were able to do it really well.

She had been irritated, upon meeting Sylvie six months prior and answering the "What do you do?" question, when Sylvie had replied, "That sounds like something I could pick up in my spare time. Why don't you teach me?"

As if it were a spare time thing. As if Maggie did this simply as a hobby between scrubbing toilets and making macaroni and cheese. Okay, so she knew that it maybe wasn't the most important job in the world, but it did serve a purpose: It helped those who wanted to sell in selling and it helped those who wanted to buy, in buying.

Here's how it worked: Show Maggie a photo of a lamp with a pedestal of four deer hooves and a plastic shade with three photos of a deer in the woods in various seasons and she would then produce a description for you, which was guaranteed (or your money back) to bring in at least 15% more than you would get had you written it yourself:

Away to the woods! Hear the gentle hoof beats of the mighty buck. See his rack, gleaming ivory in the rich green woodlands. He spots you, snorts and is away, just a white tail whisking through the grove. Keep him with you forever now in the comfort of your study. Read by his glow. Starting bid: $49.95

Maybe it wasn't as lofty as motherhood, but it certainly wasn't easy. It certainly wasn't spare time. It required an ability to wordsmith and a broad knowledge of antiques, of kitsch, of couture, of craftsmanship. Maggie had worked hard at building her in-home business and she'd be damned if she was going to just give that knowledge away to Sylvie for free. Let her go out and make contacts with the area antique dealers. Let her go and learn HTML and build a web site. Let her establish close and trusting relationships with some of the most active participants on eBay. Let her read books upon books on the psychology of shopping and addictive personalities. Let Sylvie do all that and then maybe they'd talk.

But instead Sylvie waited. And the boys, who could have played anywhere on the street, chose to play in the mucky culvert across from her modest cape, driving Maggie to distraction and keeping her from her work.

Eventually, when Maggie did not let them in, Sylvie gave up and took the boys home. All of them, mouths open, might have been wailing or laughing. Maggie couldn't tell.

But one thing was certain: Sylvie would be back.

*

When her mother called, as she did almost daily to check on her, to make sure she was holding up, was okay, Maggie heard the background din of the television with one of her shows on, something boisterous. People fighting with such venom that she could barely make out what her mother said so eager was she to hear their argument. Her mother said something about the new neighbors. How did Maggie like them? And when Maggie told her about Sylvie and her discomfort, her mother asked why she would be annoyed by a woman who sounded perfectly nice?

As she'd done since childhood, Maggie answered simply, "I don't know. I just am."

And, in keeping with the time honored tradition, her mother said, "Why must you be such a recluse? It's not healthy."

But to Maggie it was healthier than the alternative.

*

What Maggie had liked about the house when the realtor showed it to her in mid-May was that out each window she could see green: pine trees, hemlocks, oaks, swamp maple. Even when the leaves of the deciduous trees were gone, the evergreens hovered around the edges of her perception. She decided to carry it through to the interior and paint the walls of her bedroom green. She chose a color called Fern, invoking walks over pine needles and then stumbling, stumbling into the cool part of the forest where the gentle leaves curled up to her, reaching through the rusty pine needles and pulling her down into the cool and the wet.

It was what she wanted. To see herself in this small house alone. No others. No children to bog her down. No relationships. No others to talk to or listen to. No others to worry over. Her relationship with her most recent lover Jesse had ended a few months prior and Maggie was fine with that. When Jesse had wanted to adopt a child from Russia, Maggie, simply, had not. The thought of the child crying for her in the night. Wanting her, needing her. She felt choked with the thought of it.

"You were never open to anyone," Jesse said on that last day of packing. "You could only see the walls around you and never the faces." Maggie hardly ever missed Jesse, rarely thought of her even though they'd been together for three years.

As she opened her first paint can with the plunk-plunk of the lid, the doorbell rang. Peeking out the bedroom window from up above with no curtains to hide her because she'd taken them down for painting, she saw Sylvie on the stoop. Sylvie looked up, waved, sent her kids to the tire swing, a remnant of the previous owners which Maggie kept out of a sense of latent hopefulness, which she could not place. Sometimes, though, it depressed her to see the thing swaying, empty in the wind on a gray day, rain pelting into the soft ground.

She took her time putting the lid back on the paint, wiping off her hands. She just wanted to paint her quiet room. Wanted to listen to the unaccompanied cello suites. Wanted Sylvie to go away and if she would not go away, wanted her to die.

But Sylvie saw her and so Maggie had no choice but to let her in. It was her own fault that Sylvie wanted to see her.

*

Initially, she wondered what it was that so fascinated Sylvie. What made her come back again and again. Sylvie's husband, too, was interested, although in a less insidious way. From the beginning both of them peppered Maggie with questions that never really got to the point. She knew they were desperate to find out why she was alone.

Instead, their questions were more like statements, "Your husband is going to love all the painting you've done" and "I bet your children will love to ride their bikes here." Until they became so irritated or bored by Maggie's reticence that they spoke only of themselves. As she learned of them, she created a mental eBay listing:

> *Neighbors aren't just folks to wave at over the fence anymore. Meet John and Sylvie—and meet them you will as they share intimate details of their lives with you. Learn how they met*

freshman year at BU and have been together ever since, except for that one summer when John accidentally fucked Sylvie's cousin and they took a time out. Learn how Sylvie dropped out of the workforce because she wanted to be a mother more than anything. Learn how they almost went bankrupt when John was laid off two years ago and how they have risen from the ashes with his new high six-figure salary. Learn of their two boys— Tucker and Marshall—and how they are considered "advanced" by their teachers and peers. Don't even bother trying to bid on these neighbors, because the opening bid is priceless.

Maggie had also learned that Sylvie would have liked—was, in fact, bursting—to start a book club with Maggie, the thought of which turned Maggie's stomach. The idea of a group of the neighborhood women— some menopausal and podgy, others fertile and manicured, glowing from their daily yogalates classes—sitting around in a bright living room on overstuffed chairs, sipping Sauvignon Blanc and discussing Gabriel Garcia Marquez was excruciating to Maggie. She would be meant to engage, to discuss and worst of all to listen to these women. Their thoughts, their voices, their fucking opinions clawing at her like an eagle on a liver. She wanted no friends.

"And then we could maybe branch out to some of the other subdivisions and make it even more interesting," Sylvie said when she and John had Maggie over for dinner.

Maggie wondered over how to evade something as innocuous as a book club.

"You say that you are a voracious reader?" Maggie asked and Sylvie nodded, encouraged. "What's your output?"

"I'm sorry?" Sylvie said with a quick glance at John and a smile like she'd missed the joke.

"Your output? You know. If you are voracious then you eat the books." Maggie pantomimed eating for her to make it perfectly clear. "And so what do you output?"

"Uh."

"Typically, one would think that you would excrete some sort of waste product." Maggie smiled.

They both stared at her and she wondered if she might be going too far. Showing her cards a bit too soon. They'd only been neighbors for a few weeks and it was nice, she supposed, of them to ask her to dinner, even if she would rather have eaten alone in her empty house.

"Waste product?"

"From eating a meal voraciously." Maggie ate a large bite of her stew as an example. "One outputs fecal matter." Swallowed. "So what is your output from reading a book voraciously?"

"Oh," Sylvie said and slapped John on his hand. Then she laughed in ha ha ha way. "Well, I suppose my output is ideas. Ideas about life." Her hands circled the air above the table.

"Okay." Maggie grabbed another piece of bread.

"Life and, uh, art. And beauty and, I guess, truth."

"Okay!" Maggie said. Slapped her thigh. "Good."

Sylvie smiled like she'd won the forensics championship. Maggie sat back, hand on her full belly, feeling like she dodged a bullet.

That was until John asked her, "Are you married?"

And there it was. The question. Lying out in the middle of the table as inappropriate as if John had stood up and flashed his penis at her.

"John," Sylvie said.

Maggie held up a hand. "No. It's okay," she said and maybe the third glass of wine had gotten to her then because the thing that had been growing inside her for a while took shape. Maggie looked at their faces: John's, smug and Sylvie's, desperate. The sad, lonely thing flopped itself out of her mouth and lived. "My husband's gone," she said and when they did not respond. "He left me." Still nothing. "And took my son."

"Oh dear," Sylvie said, hand on throat.

"They have gone underground." Maggie sat back in her chair, reached for the wineglass. "They are missing." The thing ran around the table waving its arms, gave John the finger, mooned Sylvie, circled back and climbed up on Maggie's shoulder, her little pet, her little lie. "They are lost."

*

"Hello," Maggie said as she opened the door to Sylvie.

"Busy?" Sylvie moved her body into the door with the soft, lumpy push of a golden retriever.

"Well…"

"I won't stay long. Just let me warm up." She was in; gloves off, green jacket hung on the banister. Time after time, Maggie'd hung it up in the coat closet after she'd done just this, but had since given up. Let it stay on the banister, then. Let it stay.

"It's freezing out," Sylvie said rubbing her hands together. "Feels like snow." Sylvie led the way into the kitchen where Maggie kept a carafe of coffee filled, got cups down, poured two coffees--left Maggie's black but got some 2% milk from the fridge for her own.

"So," Sylvie said, sitting on one of the stools at the center-island. "How's it going?" She blew on her coffee and looked over the mug at Maggie.

Maggie shrugged, smiled, picked up her coffee and stared into it.

"Good then?" Sylvie asked.

Maggie puzzled over what to say because the last time they'd seen each other had been emotional.

After their dinner, Sylvie had been ever the eager shoulder to cry on, offering Maggie time and again a chance to talk, to let it all out. But Maggie had been speechless, fearful she'd be caught in her lie, annoyed that Sylvie would not just let it go and annoyed at herself for allowing the thing to live in the first place.

Maggie hadn't meant to keep it going but she had felt she had no choice when Sylvie, who had brought in Maggie's post from the box at the end of the driveway, slipped one piece of mail into her pocket.

"What's that?" Maggie said.

Sylvie, wide-eyed, said, "Nothing."

"I saw you put something in your pocket," Maggie said.

"Oh Maggie, it's nothing. Junk mail."

"If it's nothing, then give it to me." Maggie held out her hand.

Reluctantly, Sylvie pulled a crumpled bit of paper out of her pocket. It was one of those fliers with the missing children and their abductors. Across the top it said, "Have you seen us?" Maggie clapped her hand to her mouth to stifle a laugh. Sylvie mistook Maggie's expression for horror and threw her arms around her, squeezing tightly.

"It's all right," Sylvie said. "It is all right. Just let it out. You'll feel better."

Maggie had stood rigid in those arms. Her mind processing where to go next. What to say. To go deeper or to push it off.

"He was only four," Maggie said, letting go. "Just four." And as the warmth of Sylvie's embrace softened her, she felt wetness upon her cheeks. Feeling the fourness of the child. His smell, milky, vulnerable. His soft, pudgy arms around her neck. His cheek against hers.

"I'm so, so sorry," Sylvie said, rocking her now, a baby. "So sorry." Maggie slumped farther into the arms and rested there on Sylvie's shoulder. She liked the way it felt. To be cared for that way. She felt that she could be alone, even there, in Sylvie's arms.

Over time, though, she had begun more and more to resent these visits from Sylvie. They became less the breakthrough moment of joining together in grief and more the meals-on-wheelsie, visiting pastor sort of visits. The pull yourself up by your bootstraps and carry on. And, horrifyingly, the what can we do as a community to help you find your child. Can we get *Unsolved Mysteries* in? Can we get *America's Most Wanted*?

Maggie had felt less fearful at these suggestions and more as though Sylvie was not taking care with her information. She had started to feel as though Sylvie was using her.

The last time, then, that Sylvie had sat in Maggie's kitchen, Maggie had lost it.

It wasn't a game. It wasn't at all funny, ha ha, or funny strange. And Sylvie didn't know. Couldn't possibly. How, after all, could Sylvie understand the overwhelming sense of disconnection at the loss of a child? The feeling that your body is being split into a million, billion particles and scattered to the wind? How could that be understood by someone who had not been violated in such a way?

Didn't Sylvie know that Maggie had already done everything, e-ver-y-thing in her power to find her boy and bring him home? Didn't Sylvie know that each time she mentioned a new plan she reopened the wound in Maggie's gut, letting it all spill out and fester again? Couldn't she see that?

Sylvie, she felt, was not deserving of her grief. And all of this was what she had said to Sylvie the last time they had seen each other.

Sylvie had been devastated. "But Mag," she said, "I know." She reached for Maggie's hand and gripped it. "I can't imagine how I would feel if I lost my boys." Maggie had looked down at her hand in Sylvie's. A hand in a hand. Yes. We share this. If we lost our boys we would be devastated.

Then Maggie felt a curtain of skin move over the two them, enwrapping them in the middle of Maggie's kitchen. Their bodies seemed to move closer, forehead to forehead. Maggie felt joined together in this womb of understanding. Felt the twin-ness of Sylvie.

She had squeezed Sylvie's hand and met her eye. "Yes," Maggie said.

*

The boys came to the back door and stood, staring in, faces red with cold. Sylvie saw them and held a finger up in a "just a minute," eager to finish her story. Maggie moved to get up to let the boys in but Sylvie held a hand out, palm facing her to keep her put.

Sylvie finished telling about her plans for the Christmas holidays (Cayman Islands for Sylvie and John) and then she got up to let the boys in, talking all the while as she removed their mittens, hats, scarves, and jackets. She unzipped their boots and let them sit on the floor to take them off themselves. Still talking, saying something but Maggie didn't hear her.

Her boys were there and the world opened up. "Would you like cocoa?" Maggie said to them over Sylvie.

"No, they're fine," Sylvie said.

"They're so cold," Maggie said, crouching down and taking one pair of small hands in hers. "Wouldn't a little cocoa be nice? With marshmallows?" The boy nodded when his mother wasn't looking.

"Really," Sylvie said, as she stood up and stretched her back. "Don't go to any trouble for them."

"No trouble," Maggie said. "None at all." She winked at her boys when Sylvie busied herself hanging up their things on the pegs by the door and they smiled. Their tiny, bright coats hanging against the white walls stung Maggie then. She took a step back and breathed in quickly, her hands flapping to her chest.

Sylvie went to her, placed her hands so competently on Maggie's arms and looked into her eyes. "Are you okay? Do you need to sit?"

"No," Maggie said resolutely. "I'm fine. It's just a muscle twinge." The boys looked scared though. Maggie tried to bring them back to her. "Boys, I've got the television set up for you in the other room, with some cushions and blankets." They brightened, scooted by in stocking feet, racing to see who would get the remote control.

Maggie busied herself with their cocoa, preparing to broach an uncomfortable subject with Sylvie. She wanted to say that while Sylvie and John were on vacation the boys could stay with her. That she would make their breakfast and take them to school. Would make their lunches and dinners and give them baths and tuck them in. She would be just like their mother. She was just going to have to go ahead and say it.

"I was thinking."

"Yes," Sylvie said, leaning forward. "Yes, what were you thinking?" She was so eager that Maggie almost lost her nerve or maybe her desire.

"Oh nothing."

"Come on," Sylvie said, grabbing Maggie's hand. "Tell me."

The touch of skin emboldened her. "It's nothing. It's silly."

"Oh go ahead."

"Well, I wanted to say that if you haven't found a sitter for when you're on vacation that I'd love to watch the boys."

"Ohhhh," Sylvie said. "Oh. I mean, it's so nice of you to suggest it. Really. But they're staying with John's mother."

"Well, I just thought with school and such, it would be easier."

"Oh you are sweet to think of that but it's vacation—so no school and besides Mim would be devastated not to have her boys staying with her." Sylvie smiled. "But thank you. I really mean that and maybe next time."

Maggie felt cold, blank. "Okay." She turned to the cocoa and for a moment, silence. Didn't want to think of Sylvie's eyes on her. Wished they would all leave.

Maggie spun from the stove with the bubbling pot of cocoa in her hand, moved in the direction of Sylvie.

"It would have been nice if you'd thought of me to take care of the boys," Maggie said.

"Maggie," Sylvie said leaning back, away from her. "I don't know what to say."

Maggie couldn't trust herself to speak. Felt the grief of the lost child wave over her, encompassing. She put the pan down and pinched her nose, wiped at her eyes.

"It's just that you know it will be my first holidays since..."

Sylvie looked stricken, grabbed Maggie's arm. "I'm sorry," she said. "That was insensitive of me."

Maggie poured the cocoa into cups and sprinkled them with marshmallows.

"Boys," Maggie called out harshly. In response, the television blared cartoons in the other room.

"I think..." Sylvie said.

"What?"

"It might be too hot for them right now."

"I know," Maggie snapped. "I know what I'm doing." She yearned to throw the cocoa in Sylvie's face.

Sylvie's eyes twitched, her mouth opened, shut, hands gripping her coffee mug and she seemed to be looking for escape.

"Boys," Maggie called again. Movement from the other room and then the two of them were before her. Maggie smiled. "I've got a question. Okay?" They nodded.

"Maggie," Sylvie said.

Maggie ignored her. "Okay, here's my question: who would you rather spend Christmas holidays with, nice, fun, Maggie who will give you lots of treats and let you stay up and sleep in or mean old Mim who will make you eat Brussel sprouts and go to bed at seven?" The boys glanced at their mother, giggled nervously.

"Maggie, that's enough," Sylvie said, racing around the counter and facing off with Sylvie and the boys. "Boys, get your clothes on. Time to go home."

"But their cocoa," Maggie said, a hand on each boy's head.

Sylvie grabbed the boys by the arms and pulled them to her. "The cocoa will spoil their dinner." She pushed the boys toward the door. "It's time for us to go," she said.

"What? Why?" Maggie reached for her—for the hand that had held hers before but Sylvie moved away, looked like she might cry.

"I just don't know, Maggie," Sylvie sighed. "Listen, I know you're hurting and I'm sorry for that, I am."

"You're not sorry," Maggie said, poking at Sylvie where she was most vulnerable, her guilt.

"I am sorry," Sylvie said. "But I can't have you treating my boys that way."

Our boys. Not your boys. Ours.

"I wish you had your boy back," Sylvie said. "Wish it more than anything in the world but you can't replace him with my sons."

Mine.

"I'm sorry," Sylvie said. "Maybe you should find someone to talk to. Someone who understands. A support group or a therapist or something"

"I don't need to, "Maggie said. "I've got you."

"Yes, you do and I want you to know that I'll always be there for you, Maggie but I've been thinking that maybe we should take a break from seeing each other for a while. A time out." Sylvie took Maggie's hand but the grip felt cold, felt not like it was coming together but that it was falling away. "I just need some time away from all of your... stuff. I'm sorry. I wish I were stronger but I'm not. Please forgive me." Sylvie leaned forward, kissed Maggie on the cheek and left.

Maggie watched the green jacket and the blue and the red as they rounded the corner and were out of sight.

The cocoa sat, untouched on the counter, marshmallows congealed in a dingy, sticky lid. Maggie took a sip, gagged on the sweetness of it, and dumped it down the drain. She ran the disposal for ten full minutes.

*

Maggie took her walks later and later in the morning. When she first moved in she was happy to be out before sunrise, but she found getting out of bed early was disagreeable in the dim morning light of January and February, especially since she spent so many late nights in front of her computer. Walking one morning, she saw Sylvie at the bus stop with the boys. Sylvie, chatting with some of the other mothers, didn't notice Maggie, but the boys did and when they saw her, looked down, away.

Maggie frowned and was about to cross the street to talk to them when the bus pulled up. She watched as the children got on and found seats. Stood there as the last child sat and the bus pulled away. The mothers who had been standing behind it were gone.

Weeks passed and there was no word from Sylvie. No sight of the boys. Maggie took to driving by the bus stop every morning just so she could be sure they were all right.

Finally, Sylvie spotted her but did not wave. In the rearview, Maggie saw her green jacket, hands on hips, watching.

*

Maggie's mother called to tell her that she heard from Jesse. When Sylvie said, "Who?"

Her mother, incredulous, replied, "Your ex." They had been close, her mother and Jesse. "She's like the daughter I never had," her mother said once as a joke. Maggie had not laughed.

"She's having a baby," her mother said.

"Having?" Maggie said, sitting in front of her computer and typing fuck, fuck, fuck you over and over again into an empty text file. "Having?"

"Oh, you know what I mean," her mother said. "Getting one."

"Oh?"

"Adopting one. From Russia."

Maggie tried to picture Jesse with the Russian baby in her arms but instead, she thought of Sylvie and her boys in their cozy home. Thought of Sylvie curled up before the fire reading a book voraciously. Maggie hung up on her mother as she went through the tedious details of Jesse's adoption story.

She got her coat on and walked to Sylvie's house. Sylvie answered the door, dressed in fleece. "Hi, Mag," she said, shutting the door a little bit so that it was clear she wouldn't be asking Maggie in. "We're just about to sit down to dinner."

"Really?" Maggie said. "It's only four."

"The boys are eating early tonight," she said. "What can I do for you?"

"I wanted to talk to you about the book club." Maggie smiled.

Sylvie looked at her watch. "Now's really not a good time. How about I drop by next week?"

"When?" Maggie put a hand on Sylvie's door then, almost threatening to push it open. To enter. And do what, she wondered. Would she throw Sylvie down and embrace her? Would she grab the boys and run?

Sylvie looked at Maggie's hand and pulled at the neck of her top. "How about we say Wednesday?"

"Okay. See you Wednesday then."

"Good," Sylvie said and shut the door another hair. "I've really got to get cracking," she said.

"Okay. Right. So Wednesday."

Sylvie shut the door a bit more but Maggie couldn't make herself turn around and leave. Just one glimpse of the boys. The boys and Sylvie together.

"Okay, bye," Sylvie said and shut the door. Maggie's navel contracted, then, sucking in, pulsing. Wanting to pound on the door, she turned and headed for home instead.

*

Wednesday came and there was no Sylvie and not on any of the Wednesdays that followed either. Maggie's mother called her almost nightly, telling her more news about Jesse and the baby. How she was doing it alone. How brave. How strong.

"She'd take you back, you know," her mother said. "Jesse would take you back. Then you wouldn't be alone." And the unsaid, and I wouldn't have to worry, rang in Maggie's head.

Maggie wanted to say to her, "I don't need to be back." Wanted to say, "I have my family."

But she wasn't sure she really did. Sylvie had taken to driving the boys to school and Maggie followed her Volvo and watched as the boys entered the school and then in the evening when they ran back out of it, waving drawings or report cards in their hands.

Her heart filled with all of their joy and she laughed as they laughed.

*

In March, a "For Sale" went up on Sylvie's lawn. Then Maggie saw an open house listed for several weekends in a row. Then the sign said, "Sale Pending" and finally, "Sold."

On a warm spring day, Sylvie, John and the boys took a final walk around the cul de sac. They stopped, chatted with other neighbors but they never came down Maggie's driveway. The boys looked happy, glad to be moving to their new home. They ran into the culvert and Sylvie took off her green jacket, tying it around her waist. John pulled her close around the shoulders, kissed her.

As Maggie watched, the green jacket slipped undone and fell. The kiss ended and they called the boys and headed home as a group while the jacket lay in the middle of the street. All day Maggie watched it, waiting for someone to come back and get it. When no one had by dusk, she retrieved the jacket, scanning the area as if looking for its owner and then shrugging and bringing it back to her house. She forced herself to walk at a normal pace, hugging the jacket tightly, tightly to her chest.

Inside, she held it up by the shoulders and embraced it. Up the stairs in her green room she placed the jacket, carefully, on the bed. Before it, she removed her clothes, one item at a time with slow, simple seduction. Naked, she slipped into Sylvie's jacket, feeling the warmth of it from where her limbs had touched it, from how they had reached around her boys to hug them, to pull them close. Maggie wrapped her arms around herself, feeling so close.

OBTUSE,
NOT
EQUILATERAL

All winter long, the dog looked off into the woods and barked more often than normal. There was something out there. Most likely it was deer.

Sitting in her office, a pillow on her chair to placate her sciatica, Lila read online that a hundred years ago there were half a million deer in the United States. Today, there was something like 20 million deer.

Still each time she saw one it was still like a special gift. The fragile-legged fawns.

Once, she'd seen a starving deer while she hiked in Bryce Canyon. It had been too lethargic with want to run from her, just stood and stared at her with what looked like a festering teen angst. She'd told a park ranger about the deer but he advised her to let it go. There was no saving the creature. The world was tightening around the deer, expanding and contracting in equal time, forcing them closer and pushing them farther away.

*

The backyard was a glacier. Snow piled upon snow, crusty and brick-hard. The dog skittered around like a crab, seeking out rough ground to cling to.

But the birds were lightening; the gold and house finches starting to show their bold color again. There was hope. And the news that a boy in

Lila's neighborhood had taken part in a murder in late September was beginning to fade for most people, but Lila could not forget. In fact, she felt she might be a part of it. That it was her fault in some narcissistic way she could not comprehend.

Here were the facts: This boy and his friends had broken into the Greek Revival home of a young couple and stabbed the husband with knives from his kitchen and beat him with the hammer from his toolbox. They killed him. The wife was left alive, though barely. Beaten and raped, one of her neighbors found her tied to her bedpost.

Lying in her bed at night, listening to the wind roll hard and low over the salt marsh, Lila thought of her wrists bound, her legs puddled beneath her. How her heart would beat and push the blood out of her body swamping the carpet, so carefully picked out to match the pale stripe in her accent pillows.

*

The murderer boy's family were neighbors to her, though she'd never spoken to them, only noted them as a cast of characters: mother, father, son, daughter.

When she first heard the news, Lila printed a map of town off Google and taped it up to the wall in her office. She marked her house with a yellow pushpin, the murderer's house with black, and the victims' house with red.

The line from the murderer's house to her house was closer than the line from either her house or the murderer's house to that of the victims.

The lines formed a triangle. Obtuse, not equilateral.

TEMPORARY

They moved into the temporary house on an October day when the brisk wind spilled in high and white from the sea. They were told that the nearly dismantled water tower in the parking lot across the street would soon be re-erected and made to look like a windmill.

Each day, the hard-hatted men soldered, orange sparks littering the sky.

The high, white sky.

Everywhere, there were pit bulls, walking unleashed out of stores, pushing against their chain-link fences.

Dance clubs sat empty and unblinkered. Houses remained boarded and the air carried a slight tinge of natural gas, cabbagey and raw.

As they lay in their borrowed beds, they would remember the owls weeping out on winter nights, would remember spring with its hopeful peepers and the wood thrush calling so thrillingly from the edges of a darkened wood at the cool dawn of June.

One afternoon in November two horses galloped the beach. A balloon drifted untended by the edge of the shore. In the distance a crane worked on bolstering up a building worn raw by the coming and going of the tide.

Everything, it seemed, was crusted over and shorn.

SENNENHUND

I made the mistake of asking if his dog was a mutt, but he informed me that no, his dog was not a mutt. His dog was an Entlebucher Mountain Dog.

Do you know the Bernease Mountain Dogs? he asked.

Yes. He sort of looks like one. I bent and tried to pet the dog, but it backed away, growling.

Exactly, he said. He's the smallest of the Sennenhunds. The Bernease is the largest. The moon was out, my hot breath smoked up into the sky. I was shoveling out the mailbox when he stopped. Actually, he was pleasant, this man, and I knew the dog well. Had yelled at it, in fact, many times when it chased me as I went on my run. I bent to pet the dog, pretending that I was nice and not the woman who shrieked at him and his wife when their dog growled at me in the street. The dog shrunk away from my hand, unsure.

It's my first dog, the man said.

No dogs as a child? I said and leaned against my shovel.

My mother had a bad experience, he said and did not elaborate. I pictured her backing away from dogs as they walked along the sidewalk. I saw her calling to him from the house, stay away from that dog. She was scared.

I knew about being scared. When I was a child we'd had a neighbor who had a phobia of dolls. We girls were under strict instruction not to bring our dolls out when Geeta was over for coffee.

In the basement, we would dare each other to walk through the room where Geeta was with a doll in our hands. The cruelty of children circles around humor.

I was always the chosen one. The youngest, I was also the least full of guile. Mostly, I was excited by the task. I wanted to see what would happen. So I did it.

I brought a doll into the living room during a party. Geeta backed up into the couch cushions, clutching at her husband's arm, turning away. I felt the power of my presence. Another time, I brought a doll up the stairs from the basement while she visited with my mother in the kitchen. Geeta stood when she saw me and backed up to the door, her hand scrabbling for the handle.

My oldest sister had a nun doll. I kept it in the top of my closet and only dared touch it when I felt the world was most in order. I liked to lift up the heavy black fabric and see the smooth pink skin beneath. I would look into its glass eyes and imagine what Geeta would do if she saw it.

One of my sisters told us she'd learned why Geeta was afraid. There had been a fire in her house when she was a child and she had been trapped in her closet with her dolls, waiting for someone to find and save her.

I liked to pretend I was Geeta. I sat in my closet with the nun doll and pulled closed the door. I waited for the fire. The warmth. The doll's eyes lighting from within. The light coming to greet me.

I knelt down to the dog's level and he maneuvered himself behind his master's legs.

He's skittish, the man said. I saw that the dog was scared. He would not hurt me.

It's okay, I said. I won't hurt you.

The man lifted his skittish dog up to me so that I might pet it. I took off my glove and felt its fur, soft as a puppy. The dog's eyes searched for mine. I saw his fear aching away then, melting in our hot breath. He knew me now.

I wanted to tell the man about the dog that chased me when I was a child. A German shepherd owned by a childless Iranian couple. I often saw them through the cracks in their tall hedges, he sitting in a lawn chair smoking while she worked on the garden. In anticipation of the dog, I would start to run at the sign at the top of the street: Stop. The dog circled behind me, following but not fast enough to catch me.

The man put his dog down and it looked up at him, waiting for direction. I readied my shovel. The man smiled and said goodbye and they walked away, leaving me to study the prints they'd left.

I never looked into the face of the dog that chased me in my childhood. I kept my fear closed up and hidden. Had I looked, I might have seen that he was trying to make sure I made it home safely. Not a lamb to his wolf, I was a part of the flock.

POINSETTIAS

There were four empty tins of peppermint Altoids in the cup holders in Mandy's 4-runner. On her center island in the kitchen, an empty tin of cinnamon. On the back of the toilet in the en suite, another tin of peppermint. You could find one in just about every room of the house.

She wasn't willing to admit that she had a problem. She just didn't want her mouth to taste like shit. All of these people were walking around with shit-tasting mouths, but not her. Breathe in, minty. Breathe out, fresh.

The real problem was that Nic would not let the poinsettias die. That was the problem. The real problem. Not Altoids.

It was two months past Christmas and the poinsettias should have long been plopped into the trashcan. Mandy hated buying disposable plants like that, but what was one to do? Nic enjoyed a splash of color at the holidays and who was she to deny him that? Plus, she'd bought them on sale on Christmas Eve when she'd gone to the supermarket to exchange the turkey that had gone rotten in their fridge for a fresh one.

The turkey smelled like sulfur in the fridge and it took her the longest time to figure out which thing it was that smelled so. She threw out root vegetables, cheese, strawberries. Finally, she asked Nic, "You don't think it's the turkey, do you?" He didn't think so but good thing she Googled it.

It was the damn turkey. Rotting poultry smelled like what? That's right. It smelled like sulfur.

She drove the carcass to the market in the way back of her car with the windows cracked, but even now, weeks later, the smell lingered, sulfur twisting up her nostrils.

After Christmas, Nic took over the care of the poinsettias, placing them in the sunniest room. Watering and pruning them. Some of the leaves browned and fell off, but mostly the things just thrived.

It was disappointing. She had moved on from Christmas and was looking toward spring. There was no place in spring for poinsettias.

· She supposed that maybe the Altoids had been a reaction to the poinsettias. Maybe they were a passive-aggressive get back aimed at Nic. Whenever he found one of the empty tins he held it up and examined it as if he'd never seen one before. Then he placed it in his soft palm and eased his arm in her direction. "What's this?" he said.

Mandy shrugged, frowned. "I've got to fold the laundry," she said, or something of that sort.

Each time he found a tin, the same damn thing. She was running out of non sequiturs.

The next time he held a tin up to her she gave up the shrug, the frown and asked, "Is it possible to run out of non sequiturs?"

"The poinsettias are dying," he said and lowered the tin so that he held it cupped in his hand. He brought her to the dining room where the plants sat three in a row on the table. Their leaves drooped, the red dulled of color.

Mandy touched one leaf with the tip of her pointed finger and it drifted away from the stem, landing without sound on the tablecloth.

"What happened?" She picked up the leaf, examined it, the beauty of its veins.

"Things die," Nic said.

At the supermarket, they told her they would put the rotting turkey carcass in the renderer. They would take care of it, they told her. She felt some responsibility that the flesh of the bird be taken care of, that it be brought gently back to earth, to replenish, to renew. She remembered that when her mother died, hospice had said it was okay to send a personal item with her in the ambulance on the way to the crematory. She chose a fleece, duck-covered blanket that her mother had always snuggled under. That blanket was soft. It was so soft. When she thought of the flames, it was not her mother's body she saw, but that blanket pushing toward the heat.

COCKFIGHT

All that was left of the hermit crab was its shell. She'd enjoyed watching it scrabble around in its tank. Liked to think it was happy there with her but perhaps it had been desperate for food or escape. Maybe it had dried into dust and blown away. She picked up the shell and examined the interior. Lifted it to her ear.

Where did you go? she asked.

On impulse she looked outside. A couple of male robins fought on the woody edge of the lawn. One leapt backward, retreating. The other flew mercilessly forward, pecking and clawing.

On their honeymoon, her husband had brought her to a cockfight. The dusty alley. A man chewing on a chicken leg beckoned them into a tin-sided building. "Where do we go?" her husband asked. The man used the chicken leg to point them to a separate room, lit by fluorescence.

She supposed he thought it would be interesting for her. So foreign and raw. Not a bull fight, but close. Instead, it had left her stricken and unable to leave their room for the final few days of their trip. All of that blood and horror and the men cheering. The dying creature ran headless around the ring before collapsing and convulsing in the dirt.

Afterward, she lay in their honeymoon bed with the curtains closed against the tropical sun. She considered her soul. How, in an attempt to flee, it would stretch forth like a rubber band only to snap back and remain tethered to her. Her soul was not boundless. It was as attached to her as was her own head. She could not crawl out. There was no end.

ASK
FOR
THIS

Those walking through found the house smelled of someone gone, weedy and dank.

How would they know he sat on the cement floor of his basement and regarded her name penciled on the label of one of the drawers of their filing cabinet? The cabinet held their bills, their passports. It held his newspaper clippings and her garden diaries.

It did not hold the summer they met.

It held nothing.

Wolfeboro: They worked at the same resort on Winnipesauke. His second summer, her first. Gosh, she was pretty. Black hair and puckered lips. A real looker. His dad would think so, too, though he hoped his dad wouldn't notice everything about her.

They had bumped into each other on the shrouded lane which led to the beach. He went left, she went left. He went right, she went right. They laughed. Slapstick. No better way to break the ice.

Weeks before he dared touch her, hand on skin above her capris, just below where her knotted sleeveless blouse had ridden up. They were sitting on the dock, talking, as they did, well after all of the guests were either in bed or out dancing for the night.

Lap, lap, lap, the waves against the wood.

Their feet dangled and swung and hesitated above the water. She laughed at something he said and tipped her body backward. He reached out to steady her, the palm of his hand tissuing her smooth back.

He remembered that his hand on her back had lingered.

But it had not. His hand was a hummingbird, alighting, and off.

Ask for this:

Alighting, alighting.

Off, off.

Alighting.

Ask for this hand, a hummingbird.

PRAYER

I think of the woods and of losing you there and of the dark path that leads down to the cottage where I was walking when a half-dozen gray and silver wolves surrounded me. Some showed their white teeth and others just stared. I was full of fear, fearful; there was nowhere for me to go.

When the dark trees cover the lawn with their velvet light and the shadows slither across the grass but high above them one can still see the blue sky and the sun shining somewhere--that is when it is time to go out into the woods and look for the path that leads to the lake; the lake that you live on; the lake that will drown you if you let it.

Do not let it drown you.

Follow, follow, follow and breathe and do not let the wolves get you and do not let the lake drown you. Just follow and follow and it will lead you.

It will lead you to where we are born anew and we go to our lives, where forgetting and remembering become the same thing.

We are not so much born as we are remembered.

Let's go back to the woods. Let us go to the woods and build a garden with a rock wall. I will find the rocks and haul them to you in a wheelbarrow and you can place them one by one in a puzzle that forms a wall. Let us.

Let's make each day a prayer that only we understand. Let us make each day a prayer. The ground there is dark, sodden with life remembering and forgetting. Life coming back again. It will never become that tar pit and it will never become that piece of coal. It will not petrify.

In truth, we don't know how long we have and we can't know how long we can know.

And I say this to you in my voice. This is my own voice and this is what I say to you. Let us make each day a prayer.

We will learn new words and give them meaning. We will teach each other to sing. I will show you my palm and you will kiss it.

This is the prayer today.

Let us go back to the woods.

Where the path leads to the cottage.

And the wolves surround us licking and sniffing.

And the lake, which may drown us.

Let us go there and build a wall of stone.

Which I will haul for you.

And we will teach each other to sing.

My palm, kiss it.

And we will learn new words and give them new meaning.

Let us make each day a prayer.

Let us.

Between me, you, and the rest of the world.

The mourning dove reminds me that it is not just day it is morning. The mockingbird coming home to her nest reminds me that it is time to pray.

Each day will be a new prayer with new words. You can bring them yourself or you can use the old ones. It doesn't matter to me.

I will build the wall if you can't fit the pieces together. I will build it from my memory of how it should be. I will forget and then I will remember again.

A rusty tree and wreath. A wraith. A life behind a fence is hidden to me. The ground molts and moulds. Sheds its winter skin and blinks at me. It is time.

Let us pray.

Here are your wall and your woods. Here are your fence and your shadow. Here are your wolves and your lake and your drowning (do not drown, you). Here are your forgetting and remembering and your remembering and forgetting.

If you will stay and not follow me there, I will show it all to you.

LOOK
UP.
LOOK
UP.

The technician who performed Mandy's mammogram admired her necklace. "It's my birth month moon," Mandy said, lifting the silver disk up and examining it. Gil, her mother's widower, had given her the necklace for her 35th birthday. "It's October. The bear moon."

"What about a blue moon?" the woman baby-voiced from behind the computer terminal. She had one of those high, soft voices that seems like it might be put on but as time goes on you realize that it is a real voice. "I love a blue moon," the woman said as she tucked Mandy's breast into the machine.

Mandy wasn't sure the woman understood the concept of the birth month moon. It was like a birthstone, she later thought to say when she was in her car. Regardless, the technician had moved on to some jewelry she collected. It was called dead lake or something of the sort. Mandy couldn't follow but lacked the energy to gain understanding.

"Have you had digital before?" the woman asked in between breasts.

"It's my first time," Mandy said. There had been no reason before her mother's diagnosis for such a precaution. Forevermore, Mandy would live with the knowledge that just as easily as her breasts had grown onto her body, they too could be taken away.

"Come and see," the technician invited her behind the computer where they stared at Mandy's breast tissue on the screen.

Her imaged breast resembled the moon, glowing hard on a gray night, lighting up an empty field below. Romantic.

"Isn't it great?" the woman asked.

"Amazing," Mandy said, though, as a rule, she hated the word amazing. Alone, she would have reached a hand out and touched the image. Her flesh, magnified. Lit up from within. When her mother was dying, there had been many such images. Scans of this and scans of that and dark splotches on white backgrounds. A Rorschach of illness.

"My son is a kindergarten teacher," the woman said, as they continued to examine the breast. Oh here it came. There was no ring and so everyone just assumed that her life's desire was to be shackled to another. She had no desire for a soul mate as her mother had. She wished, instead, that she had been enough for her mother; that after Mandy's father died, her mother wouldn't have needed anyone other than Mandy.

Her mother was Mandy's soul mate. There would never be another.

"He's six one," the technician said. The tall lived longer. Mandy had read that somewhere. But was that true? Maybe the short lived longer. Never mind. Her mother had been small, petite.

She thought of her mother, hairless, a sad wig and kerchief atop her head, nodding as the doctor pointed to the encroachment of black splotches. From breasts to organs to organs to organs to brain. It wasn't until she was nearly gone, until it was too late, that her mother cried, her brain covered in moss.

*

Mandy had taken the entire afternoon off work. She was to meet Xavier in Newburyport at the marina. "We'll see whales," he said. "Harmless," winking. Xavier and his wife had seven children--two sets of twins and then a set of triplets.

Jesus.

Mandy should have said no to his invitation. A whale watch was not harmless. Neither had been their trip to Plimouth Plantation, after which she was the naughty pilgrim whose butter was not properly churned. Nor was the duck tour of Boston without its pitfalls, namely a bottle of wine on the esplanade and some tricky maneuvering back into her sweater when the bicycle cop stumbled upon them. But Xavier enjoyed taking her on these kitschy, touristy outings. "You are a ray of light, Mand," he said. "You heat me up."

Despite living in New England her entire life, Mandy had been on only one other whale watch before but it had been benign. No, not benign, rather it was unsuccessful. Whales had not been watched.

She and some friends had taken the boat from Provincetown on an overcast day. The crew was determined to find them whales. They were on the boat for three hours before some of the people on board saw the sliver of the back of a whale whisper beneath the water. Then they'd headed back in. That night Mandy had gotten wasted and slept with a man who claimed to be an exiled prince from some Eastern bloc country. Her period arrived early and on his sheets and Mandy had awoken bloodied and convinced that he'd stabbed her. This man, this stranger, had had to calm her down and prove to her that it was truly her menstrual blood. She had not sought whales out since.

Xavier had told her to wear layers for their watch. It was a cool day for June, the breeze stiff and white off the ocean. She saw him leaning against his car in the parking lot, tapping furiously into his blackberry. That would be his wife, asking when he would be home for dinner or to pick up diapers or whatever the fuck she asked him twenty million times a day. It wasn't Mandy's place to discuss the messages. She had no place at all, really.

They hadn't even known each other a year. They met through Match. com and carried on a sexual relationship until Xavier admitted the truth of his life, his burden. She was sure he expected her to turn away from him, instead she had shrugged and carried on. It suited her that they would remain unfettered to each other. It suited her just fine.

And now here she was again, walking toward Xavier, a light emanating from him, cutting through and illuminating her from within. Her organs pierced white and black, blood pulsing and sluicing through her, pulling her to Xavier.

Look up. Look up. Look up now and see me.

And she knew that when he did see her, he would not look away. He would tuck his blackberry into his pocket and open his arms for her.

Had she been another person, she would have thought of his many children, raising their faces to him, opening mouths, crying for food and more than that, crying for his love and forgiveness and acceptance, his children asking that he be there, just there, but she was not another—only this one person filled with white and black. Diseased and undiseased. Loved and unloved.

She was a bear moon shining against a deep autumnal sky.

*

On her way to meet Xavier, Mandy had called Gil, hoping to get the machine. "Mandy?" he said as he picked up. "What's wrong?" He was always worried something was wrong, so much so that she sometimes thought that there might be something wrong. Terribly, terribly wrong.

They lived together. Or, they shared a house. It was the house that Gil and her mother had lived in for the three years of their marriage. Before that, the house had belonged to Gil and his wife, who died of some womanly cancer. Gil and Mandy's mother met at a widow/widower support group and never looked back. Apparently, Mandy learned, these sort of hookups were not uncommon.

Mandy sold her condo in the North End and moved in with her mother and Gil when the diagnosis came through. "We're going to need you," her mother said. "I'll need you and so will Gil. He'll have no one after I'm gone." And what of Mandy? Who would she have after her mother was gone? She hadn't asked that. It seemed a petulant question to come from a grown woman, but she could not let it go and asked herself over and over in the months that followed, Who will I have?

The house was a three bedroom Cape in Andover, close to Mandy's work. "It'll work out fine," Mandy said, holding her mother's thin cool fingers above the hospital sheet.

"Thank you, darling," her mother said, and shut her dark eyes to rest. As always, she wore lipstick and had styled her hair, even though she had been lying in a hospital bed waiting for results for two days. "Gil's awfully scared," her mother whispered, "He needs us."

Mandy was to understand that just as her father had needed them to save him from his alcoholism, so, too, did Gil need them to be his strength. Had they not just gotten the word that Mandy's mother was dying, she would have been incensed. Instead, she swallowed down her rage and saved it for later, on the drive home, ranting into her cellphone to Xavier. But it wasn't actually Xavier, rather his voicemail. He had not picked up when she called.

But that had been eight months ago, and now a few weeks after her mother's cremation, she was on her way to meet Xavier, to see whales. "They will make you believe in God," he told her by way of enticement. She wanted to believe that they would.

"Nothing's wrong, Gil," she said, stuffing her impatience down with a smile. "Wanted to let you know that I might be late."

"I was going to grill." Gil was retired and now that her mother was gone and no longer required his care, he had taken to cooking and caring for Mandy, but it wasn't the sort of care that she desired: her mother's hand stroking her hair as she leaned her head against her shoulder. Just thinking of her mother's touch conjured up the smell of her mother's cigarettes and often, inexplicably, stale armpits. Her mother always wore heels.

"I'm sorry," Mandy said. "Maybe you could save it for tomorrow?"

Gil sighed. She knew he would be running a hand over his jaw, itching behind his ear. "It's seafood," he said. Gil had a thing about seafood and corn on the cob being eaten on the day you bought them.

"Sorry," Mandy said. Now is when she should say it. She had been waiting and since he was already upset with her. Now. Say it. Say this: I'm moving out.

"Oh don't worry, sweetie," Gil said. "Tomorrow is another day." That it was, but tonight was also another night and she knew he would expect her in his bed just as she had been every night since her mother died.

Nothing was supposed to have happened between them. He had found her on their bed, weeping into her mother's pillow, her mascara spilling onto the white case. Breathing in and breathing in and breathing in the scent of her mother. She knew it would be gone soon, just as her father's laugh was gone. But she could live without her father's laugh.

She could not live without her mother, the smell of her, her cool hand, how it felt to be hugged by her.

Gil had spooned up behind her and held her and said, "I know. I know. I know." Soon he stopped saying anything and just held her and petted her head as she calmed herself. It had been afternoon, mercilessly sunny, and the next thing she knew it was night. She opened her eyes and felt strong arms holding her and knew that she was still alive. She let him turn her to face him.

And they kissed.

It was not horrible as she might have thought it would be before. Rather there was a joining together, almost a reverse birth in which her connecting with Gil brought her mother back.

I'm giving you life, she said to her mother. You are alive in me as I once was in you. It was as though she could feel her mother growing within her, a zygote, struggling to live.

Gil came quickly and then they both wept and as they wept, a kernel of hatred blossomed within Mandy. She hated herself and she hated Gil and she hated her mother for dying and leaving her there all alone and making her do this bad and awful thing with this man who was practically her father.

She saw herself as a zygote then. A zygote within the zygote, all of them replicating within each other, living on each other like parasites.

"I will not go to the desert," her mother had repeated over and over again on the nights before her death. Mandy clung to the fading sound of her mother's voice in her head as she lay beside Gil, whistling softly through his nose in exhausted sleep.

*

Xavier kept her close on the boat; he held her wedged between his thighs, his arms wrapped around her. "Let me know if you feel queasy," he whispered into her ear.

She shook her head no. She was fine. Though not really. She was still pissed at herself for not telling Gil that she was leaving, had, in fact, put a deposit down on an apartment in Salem. She had practiced what she would say, something about wanting to be closer to the sea and closer to the city. That she wanted more of an urban atmosphere. And, if it came to it, she would tell him that she needed space to grieve.

This last bit was closest to the truth. She felt that Gil had consumed her along with her grief, taken it on as his own until he was the one holding the heaviest bag of grief. "She was my soul mate," he said to her that first night. "There will never be another one for me like your mother."

Mandy had learned from her mother that Gil's first marriage had been a rocky one and that he had stayed with her purely out of duty. They were childless because of the wife's failure, Mandy learned, to produce. First her ovaries had been covered in benign cysts, causing her crushing infertility, which later turned into a womb full of tumors. That was the offspring they created. Gil, her mother assured her, was not bitter, though. "He thinks of you as his own," her mother had said to her from the hospital bed—her death bed—the hospice folks had installed in the tiny downstairs bedroom. "You should call him Dad," her mother said before drifting into a drugged and fitful sleep.

The boat lurched through the harbor, up the river, and out into the sea. Mandy felt easy, light. She felt the bulk of Gil lifting off her bones. Her grief existed in the clouds this day and not in the soil.

"Look," Xavier said, pointing in the distance. "Seals," he said.

"Aren't they lovely?" Mandy said squinting. She saw nothing but the sea before them, black and unyielding. When are you coming home? Gil had asked her. Home. The house which she lived in with him, had moved into to care for her dying mother, was not her home. She had a room there, upstairs across the hall from the master. The room had a dormer and she'd been excited upon moving in about the quirkiness of the room. It was a bright spot in an otherwise bleak situation. She thought herself a girl there. One who read Seventeen and believed in the power of love. It was a room made for pink gingham and bobby socks. Gil had helped her paint it, all the while telling her how it had been his first wife's sewing room. "It was supposed to be the nursery," he said, up on the ladder, using the roller on the ceiling, "but, well, you know. That just never happened." She had felt pity for him then, that he might have wanted a child who had never come.

Then she had believed that he was thinking of her as a daughter come home. Of what might have been. He was roughly the same age as her mother. He could have fathered her. She herself had never been pregnant but that was more out of choice. The yearning that she witnessed in so many of her peers did not exist within her.

"No chance of pregnancy?" the technician had asked her earlier in the day. She shook her head. Xavier had a vasectomy and Gil seemed just too old, not that she was a spring chicken, but she wasn't in her 70s. Okay, so it was possible that men Gil's age could father children, but no, that was not possible here. She could not be pregnant.

The sky peeled back a layer of grey and revealed a glittering sliver of sun, slicing down onto the sea, sparkling. The seals submerged and the boat lumbered on.

"Not much longer," Xavier said.

She smelled the brine and the tang of the gas from the engine. The boat slowed and everyone moved to the edge. A voice over the loudspeaker instructed them that they were at the feeding ground. They should be on the lookout, it told them. Watch for movement.

Soon there were gasps but Mandy was still without the sight of a whale. She strained her eyes and wondered if seeing a whale was something like those crazy optical illusion prints that had been so popular several years back. You were meant to stare at them until the geometric shapes turned into the picture you were supposed to see: A unicorn or a man with a gun or whatever. She had stared and stared but never seen anything other than what was there. Relax, people told her. Stop trying so hard.

She took a deep breath and willed her mind quiet, but all was noise and her mother's voice fading in and out of range.

"See?" Xavier said, grasping her shoulders. "See? See?" They were breathing together and she looked in the direction he pointed her to look.

The sea was blank, a dead eye clouded over. But beneath--beneath there was life, or so she was led to believe. So far she had seen nothing but the ever present gulls, lingering above.

Then she saw them, a mother and calf, slipping easily below the boat. They emerged on the other side, where the mother lifted her head slightly above the water and expelled through her blow hole. It was not a last breath, but a first breath, like an infant sucked from within his mother out to the air. Breathe!

Her mother's hands and feet had been cold the morning of her death and she had been unable to speak, but her eyes were aware. There had been no dramatic last breath as one expected. Instead, her mother had slid quietly into death, from one side of the boat to the other.

Another whale breeched the surface, hulking itself up and over with a tremendous splash. The viewers applauded and cheered. Mandy surprised herself by being among them—clapping, cheering, engaged in a moment of breathing and awe-filled living.

Mandy recalled a Babar book her mother read to her when she was small. Babar and Celeste had gone on their honeymoon and when their deflated balloon stranded them on an island filled with savages, they warred with the savages and won but still needed a way to escape, when, alas, a benevolent whale approached them and offered her back.

Perhaps the whale would rescue them, take them away from this boat. Away from their lives. Away from her mother. But no. That whale had abandoned Babar and his bride on a reef. It had been thoughtless, the book said. It had forgotten them.

It had left them behind.

Not this whale. Not now. It lived in this dark ocean and not in a child's book. She had glimpsed the whale's eye blinking. That it might blink. This creature.

ACKNOWLEDGEMENTS

The author wishes to thank the editors of the following journals in which these stories originally appeared:

The Nest – *Quick Fiction*

Zeus. Zeus? – *Quick Fiction*

Temporary – *Quick Fiction*

The Daughters – *Monkeybicycle* & *DZANC Best of the Web Anthology*

The Villager – *Caketrain*

Shame – *FRIGG*

Macaw – *FRIGG*

Dishes – *FRIGG*

Quarter – *elimae*

We Are Awake – *3AM*

Prey – *SmokeLong Quarterly*

Ask for This – *SmokeLong Quarterly*

Sennunhund – *Used Furniture Review*

Celestial – *juked*

He Died – *Untitled Books*

Buddhist – *Me Three*

Anointed – *Vestal Review*

I Am Holding Your Hand – *Monkeybicycle* & *The Rose Metal Press Field Guide to Flash Fiction*

Pointsettia – *PANK*

Liar – *PANK*

Cockfight – *Journal for the Compressed Creative Arts*

Let Me Go – *wigleaf*

Prayer – *Exquisite Corpse*

Mercy – *Cranky*

States of Residency – *Lilies and Cannonballs Review*

Freak Magnet – *flatmancrooked*

The White Button – *flatmancrooked* & *mixer publishing*

Verbatim – *Mississippi Review*

Wash, Dry, Fold – *Mississippi Review* & *DZANC Best of the Web Anthology*

Allergic – *Swivel*

What He Told Me – *Potomac Review*

The Emergency Contact – *The Jabberwock Review*

Have You Seen Us? – *The Kenyon Review*

Look Up. Look Up. – *mixer publishing*

You Don't Need Love – *Revolution House*

Obtuse, Not Equilateral – *Everyday Genius*

Orange Crush – *Storyglossia*

ABOUT THE AUTHOR

Myfanwy Collins lives in Massachusetts with her husband and son. Her work has been published in *The Kenyon Review, PANK, AGNI, Cream City Review,* and *Quick Fiction.* Her debut novel, *ECHOLOCATION,* was published by Engine Books in 2012.